REMOTE CONTROL

ROY POND
REMOTE CONTROL

AN ALBATROSS BOOK

© Roy Pond 1990

Published in Australia and New Zealand by
Albatross Books Pty Ltd
PO Box 320, Sutherland
NSW 2232, Australia
in the United States by
Albatross Books
PO Box 131, Claremont
CA 91711, USA
and in the United Kingdom by
Lion Publishing plc
Peter's Way, Sandy Lane West
Littlemore, Oxford OX4 5HG

First edition 1990

National Library of Australia
Cataloguing-in-Publication data

Pond, Roy
Remote control

ISBN 0 86760 121 3 (Albatross)
ISBN 0 7459 1707 0 (Lion)

I. Title
A 823.3

Cover: Michael Mucci
Printed and bound in Australia by The Book Printer, Victoria

Contents

1   The float plane   7
2   The flying jacket   19
3   The biplane   29
4   Beth Ryder   39
5   The wedding   55
6   The boat trip   69
7   The lighthouse keeper   80
8   Popper   91
9   The lighthouse   103
10 The rock shelf   115
11 Solarskin   123
12 The decision   134

1

The float plane

NICK LOOKED LONGINGLY out of the classroom window at the sky. It was a flying sky, not too windy, a few puffy clouds strung out across it.

He wanted to be out there flying, doing loops in his radio-controlled Supermarine float plane and screaming low over a shore. He hoped that the hobby shop had finished repairing his model float plane which had suffered what model fliers called a 'crackup' against a cliff. He planned to collect it after school.

Outside the classroom window, a Qantas jumbo jet lumbered into his patch of sky between clouds. Wouldn't it be fun to control it from where he sat, using a radio-control transmitter? He picked up his silver fountain pen, holding it delicately between thumb and forefinger, imagining that the pen was a control lever. He rested its end on the lid of a pen case, pretending this was the control panel of a radio transmitter that usually hung on a harness around his neck.

'Got you,' he telegraphed mentally to the pilot of the jumbo. 'I have control.' He slid the stick to one side. He saw the jumbo turn slowly in the sky like a whale rolling over on its belly. He laughed. Now he straightened her out, feeding in some elevator by hauling back on the stick. The jumbo lifted her ponderous nose. He gave her a boost of throttle and now the jumbo went into a gargantuan loop. She was cumbersome, but she could not deny the pulse of his signals. He wondered how the stewards and stewardesses were coping. They were probably serving lunch.

He tried a horizontal roll next. 'Coffee, tea or. . . ooooooer!' He imagined the stuck-on smiles of the hostesses sliding right off their faces like lunch off the tiny trays they were serving. Steak and vegetables, bread rolls and little containers of milk swirled around the cabin along with sprays of coffee and tea. He could see the white faces of scared passengers jammed against the cabin windows trying to see what had hit them. The captain, panicking, radioed for help. 'We've lost control. Something is throwing us around the sky. I think we're going in!'

But he was only playing with them. He wouldn't let them crash. He straightened the jumbo out and let her go on her way, although he couldn't resist one last victory roll before she went out of sight.

The jumbo was gone. Nick shrugged and put his fountain pen back into the pencase. He had better return to reading his book.

'Up in the clouds again, Nick Young?' his English teacher Miss Ryder said, looking up from the books she was marking at the front of the class. She took off her reading glasses. 'I think it's time you were brought down to earth. Since you obviously enjoy indulging in flights of imagination, here's another one. As extra homework, you will please write me an essay entitled "Coming down to earth". Have it on my desk by Thursday morning.' She went calmly back to marking her books as if there had been no interruption.

Nick coloured and returned to his book. Kate, a red-haired girl who sat in the desk next to his, shook her head at him disapprovingly. He saw it from the corner of his eye without turning to look at her. A few others in the class laughed. Nick didn't really mind about the essay. He enjoyed attention from their pretty English teacher Miss Ryder and she probably knew that he secretly liked writing essays for her. She admired his writing, he guessed, and merely wanted an excuse to encourage him. Perhaps she even wanted to read some more of his writing. It was a secret between them. The others didn't know about it. They thought that she was being tough on Nick for other reasons — reasons that were the talk of the whole school.

Well, he would show Miss Ryder. He liked to dream all right. He would write a flight of imagination that would truly dazzle her.

Nick liked to hang around hobby stores, especially the 'Hobby Hangar'. It was filled with model aircraft suspended on lines from the ceiling like squadrons of miniature aircraft frozen in flight. The shop was crammed with kits and engines and radio control parts and all the materials, paints, varnishes, dopes and coverings used in model aircraft construction. He used to dream that one day he'd accidentally be locked up overnight in the Hobby Hangar and have to play his way out.

He called in late that afternoon, almost at closing time, to fetch his aircraft which he had left for repairs after its crackup against a cliff.

He thought he was too late when he first looked in at the window of the shop. There was not a sign of activity inside. Where was Des, the owner? Perhaps the shop was already closed.

He groaned. Now he would be without his plane until tomorrow. He went to the glass door and gave it a testing push. It opened, setting off a bell in the shop. He went inside. The shop was empty. Was it supposed to be closed?

He hoped they had fixed his plane. Des, the owner, came out. 'Hi, Des.'

Des ignored his greeting and went to the door and locked it behind him. Then he peered out of the store window at the empty street, sweeping it with a stare from one end to the other.

'I don't mind if you lock me in here overnight,' the boy grinned. 'It doesn't scare me.'

'I've fixed your plane,' Des said tightly, turning around. 'I'll fetch it.' He went behind some plastic curtains and returned with the blue-and-white float plane. It looked perfect again.

'How much will that be?'

He seemed to pick a figure out of the air. 'Five dollars.'

'Five dollars!' the boy said.

'No charge then,' Des said irritably, looking edgy. Something was wrong. Des wasn't like this. 'Have it for nothing,' he said.

'I only meant I thought it would cost more. You had to repair a tailplane and redo the surface.'

Des, a clever, pock-marked man, who designed and constructed models himself and loved to talk in detail about work he had done, gave an impatient shrug. 'Listen carefully. I've fixed your plane for nothing and now you've got to do something for me.'

'What's that?'

'Just take care of it — very good care of it.'

'But I do. I don't usually fly it into cliffs.'

'Be careful. Above all, don't lose it. It's a very special aeroplane and others might want it. Don't part with it. Guard it well.'

The boy took the aeroplane off the counter and examined the bright new resurfacing. 'What have you done to it?'

'Fixed the broken tailplane — resurfaced it.'

'Then why is it suddenly so valuable?'

'You'll find out later. In the meantime, take especially good care of it. I want you to look after it for me until I can tell you more.'

He seemed so nervous and different that the worst thoughts came into the boy's mind. 'What exactly have you done to my plane, Des?'

The hobby shop owner looked cornered. 'You want an itemised receipt for a free job?'

'I'd like to know.'

'I've fixed the tailplane, repainted the surface and put on some dope.'

Dope. It was a well-known term used by aeromodellers. Dope was the name of a surface lacquer added to the skin of a model aircraft to provide a tough weatherproof seal. He didn't mean that kind of dope, did he? He couldn't mean. . . The idea set an alarm ringing in the boy's mind. Was Des hiding something illegal on his aeroplane?

They both jumped when there was a knock at the glass door outside the shop. 'Get out of here,' Des said hoarsely, 'fast.'

The boy took the float plane and hurried to the door. There was a man there. Des let him in. He was beaky-looking and wore a tweed cloth cap. The boy noticed that the man had clouds of puffy hair on the sides of his head below the cap.

The man gave him and his aeroplane a close look.

'Where are you going with that aeroplane?' he said.

'Cuba,' the boy said.

'Smart kid,' the man said sourly.

For some reason the boy kept looking behind him on his walk home. Did he think someone was following him? Why should he think that?

He did not go flying. He decided to take the model float plane apart to examine it. He had the house to himself, but he went to his bedroom, put the float plane on a worktable and snapped on an overhead light. He examined the plane from nose to tail, even taking off the engine cowling to inspect the little engine.

There were no drugs on his plane, he discovered. There was nothing out of the ordinary. It was just a model float plane in a fine state of repair. Dope. He was the dope for being suspicious. The bright new resurfacing on the float plane glowed innocently bright under the lamplight. He tapped the fuselage with a fingernail. It was hard and bright as a gemstone. It meant that the surface had drawn drum-tight when it dried, the way it was supposed to do. Des was an expert. Everybody knew it. He had even been used by an aeronautical company to construct scale flying models for research purposes.

But what was so special about the boy's model? Why had Des warned him to take especially good care of it?

A man dressed in flying gear walked across the sand of the cove to join Nick. His eyes were trained on the model in Nick's hands. 'Quite a toy,' he said.

'It's no toy. It's a scale model vintage Supermarine S6B and it's as difficult to fly as a real plane. The only difference is that I don't fly from the inside of the aircraft. It calls for special reflexes and pretty fancy coordination. I've seen real pilots tie themselves in knots trying to handle multi-channel aeroplanes.'

'Sure, kid.' His mouth curved scornfully. He wore a leather flying jacket and khaki pocketed pants and leather boots. The only thing missing was a leather helmet with goggles hoisted up on it like an extra pair of eyes sitting over his own. He seemed eager for action, except for one problem. His hand was wrapped in a bandage.

He saw Nick looking at it.

'I hurt my hand turning the propeller on a vintage biplane. It kicked into life and cracked the back of my fingers. Luckily it was on the first revolution. With the next spin I would have lost my fingers. Even so it's going to take a few weeks to heal.' He used his good hand to dip into his dark brown leather jacket and fish out a packet of chewing gum. The jacket creaked with the movement. He offered Nick a stick of gum and took one himself.

'No thanks,' Nick said. 'Are you a real flier?'

'Sure I'm real and yes I fly.'

'Then think about it. It's all very simple for the pilot of a real aircraft. You face the same way as your direction of flight. It's not that easy for me. When my float plane's flying towards me I have to be able to think in reverse. It's like writing in a mirror. It gets even trickier when you do aerobatics.'

'Let me see it.' The man held out his good hand. It was a hand the size of a baseball glove and just as leathery. Nick cautiously gave him the blue-and-white model float plane, a scale model of the 1931 Schneider

Trophy winner. The man hefted it thoughtfully in his hand. It had a wingspan just under two metres and it weighed over four kilos. 'It's quite an old-fashioned plane for a kid in the nineties.'

He peered into the tiny cockpit. He was a hawk-faced man with eager blue eyes that looked as if they had been narrowed from years of searching horizons. When he looked up, Nick half-expected to see the grime of flight in an open cockpit in his face along with paler rings around the eye area where his goggles had been.

'There's only one difference between you and me, kid. I don't fly for fun. I fly real missions. You can't fly missions with a dwarf plane.'

'Is that what you think? I could fly missions with my plane if I wanted to.'

He looked Nick up and down and then squinted into the miniature cockpit of the float plane. 'In this?'

'Why not?'

'You're small, but not that small.'

'I mean I could fly secret cargo, small precious things.'

'Such as?'

Nick shrugged. 'I don't know. Diamonds. Secret documents.'

'Would you ?'

'I've never been asked.'

'So you don't mind a little risk, hmm? Maybe you and I have a few things in common after all.' He looked at Nick with a brightening of respect.

Nick swelled a bit to think that a real flier could be impressed by anything he said, even if it was only a boast. 'Who are you?' Nick said.

'Just a flier.'

'I haven't met many real fliers,' Nick said. 'None in fact. But I love reading about fliers, one in particular. His name is Flite Madison, The Flier.'

'What if I said you were looking at Flite Madison in the flesh?'

'I'd laugh. He's a book hero.'

'Maybe. But the books could have been written about me. I'm just like him. I fly anything, anywhere and never ask too many questions, just like Flite Madison.'

The daring look in his eye convinced Nick that, like Flite Madison, he was not a man who asked questions before he acted.

'Wouldn't a flier ask questions if he was asked to do something mysterious?' Nick said.

The man smiled and shook his head. 'A few risks make it all the more interesting. What's the good of being a flier if you don't like risks? Stay on the ground if you want to play it safe.'

Nick caught the whiff of leather, wafted to him by a breeze that blew from behind the man. It came from the real leather flying jacket the man was wearing. It was the most marvellous piece of clothing Nick had ever seen. It had zips and pockets all over it and it glowed richly.

'You like it?' the stranger said, noticing.

'Is that a real one? I've always wanted one.'

'Then you should have one,' he said. 'Even a toy plane flier needs a flying jacket. It can be bleak out here on the shore.'

'They cost too much.'

'Maybe.' He shrugged. 'Be a good little flier and one day, who knows, you may get lucky.' The man gave

Nick a knowing wink as if he knew some secret. He handed the plane back to Nick. 'How about a bit of action? Are you going to fly this thing or not? Let me see your stuff.'

Nick took off from the cove and cut some fancy patterns in the sky to impress his sceptical new friend, throwing in a Tail Slide at the end of the performance. The pure stall was not Nick's favourite stunt because, whenever he tried it, the same thing happened. It happened now. He put the float plane into a steep climb and, with its nose still pointing up, he cut back the power. Immediately the flow of fuel slowed — so did Nick's own mental juices. His mind stalled and he watched, almost separated from events, as the aircraft under his control lost momentum and slid back on its climbing track. For a risky space of time he let the float plane drop. In time he snapped out of it and stabbed at engine, rudder, aileron and elevator controls on the box at his chest.

It was a near thing.

'You like my flying style?' Nick said to his companion.

'Not bad. But you didn't come out of that slide with much dignity. In fact you're lucky to come out of it with an aeroplane. If you'd tried that in a real Supermarine S6B you'd probably be dead because the Supermarine was a racer, not a stunt plane.'

Nick was flying back towards the cliffs to bring it down onto the cove when an updraught from the cliffs took him by surprise. He lost control as it caught the float plane, tipping it over. He watched powerlessly as his plane hit the cliff face and cut out. In slow motion it cartwheeled forlornly down to the sand at the bottom of the cliff.

'Nice touch,' his companion said. 'Now you are dead.'

The boy remembered the warning Des had given him. 'Take good care of it,' Des had said. Now he had smashed it. He ran to his plane.

He hoped it wasn't going to be an expensive mistake. He picked it up and ran his eyes over the gleaming length to check the damage. Wings okay, tail okay, fuselage undented. Just a broken propeller. Amazing. It wasn't a crash. It wasn't even a crackup. Yet it had hit the cliff at full force. The float plane was perfect. There wasn't even a dent. How was it possible? Nick looked up at the cliff. Had one of the scrubby plants on the cliff face cushioned the impact?

'Don't ever try that with a real plane,' the flier said, waving goodbye. 'Real planes don't bounce. See you around, kid.'

Nick thought a lot about the flier that night. He even dreamt about him.

The flier stepped out of the pages of an adventure book in the boy's bookshelf, filling his room with the smell of leather and aviation fuel. Together he and the man walked down to a cove in bright sunshine. The boy blinked, but not at the brightness — at the sight of his float plane. It sat on the beach. But it wasn't alone. Beside it, dwarfing it, sat a full-sized float plane, gently bobbing in the waves.

The flier turned and walked to the real, open-cockpit float plane.

'Give me a push off the beach,' he said. 'I'll show you how a real one flies.' The boy grabbed hold of a float and helped shove the float plane into the waves. The flier jumped onto one of the floats and waved to the boy, standing for a

moment in an arrested pose like an old-time pioneer hero about to depart on some spectacular solo crossing. He looked like a picture out of a history book.

Then he swung himself into the cockpit and went through some checks before starting the engine of his float plane. He put the aircraft around, facing out to sea. He taxied out beyond the breakers, turning into the wind. He gave her throttle and sent her on a darting run, her knife-edge floats slicing the sea, leaving behind a wake that spread like a sneer. The float plane's nose disdainfully lifted in a smooth, oiled take-off. Steadily she climbed over the water, levelling out at about five hundred feet, then he turned and flew low over the boy's head, rolling her wings. He held up his model float plane and rolled its wings in reply.

He watched the plane until she was a dot in the sky.

2

The flying jacket

NICK LAY ON HIS BED at the height of a storm, staring up at his radio-controlled model aeroplane that hung on a line in a suspended dive from the ceiling of his bedroom. It twisted in a draught like a lazy overhead fan.

He imagined it was a real plane above him and that a real, scaled-down pilot sat inside it at a miniaturised set of controls. Narrowing his eyes, he could almost make out the small brown blur of a face in the cockpit. It was Flite Madison, also known as The Flier, a favourite story character. The Flier was a renegade, old-time pilot who roamed the world in a float plane, putting down where adventure took him — on the Amazon, the Zambesi, the Nile, the Mississippi, the Murray River or on some Pacific island cove.

Outside, raindrops hammered on the corrugated iron roof of Nick's bluestone home. The noise of the rain on the roof seemed to swell and then change in pitch, taking on the roar of an aircraft engine. Nick shivered as the temperature dropped.

He imagined himself sitting snugly in the float plane

in a separate cockpit in front of The Flier and racing against some impossible odds.

They were on the Zambesi, racing to the edge of a waterfall in The Flier's open-cockpit float plane. Bullets from automatic small-arms fire ripped into their wings and fuselage, twanging off one of the floats. A speedboat filled with a crew of ivory poachers followed in the twin wakes of their aircraft's floats. The poachers were closing on the float plane as they raced on a path that would take them directly to the edge of the falls.

The jungle trees at the fringes of the river passed like a green, blurry crowd pressing forward to watch while ahead the thunder-smoke of the falls rose out of the gorge to meet them. They were only a few hundred metres from the lip of Victoria Falls, the mightiest waterfall in Africa. If they didn't reach air speed soon, they would enjoy one last glorious glide to disintegration along with a million tonnes of water going over into the gorge below.

He heard the engine lift in pitch as The Flier gave her more throttle. Up Flier, up, he willed the pilot behind him. He lifted his legs in anticipation, like a spectator watching a high-jump event, in the hope that it would help The Flier lift them off the river. The edge sped nearer.

Then they were over the lip of the falls, in a cloud of misty spray. Were they gliding or flying under power? There was a moment when the present blended with eternity when, like cartoon characters going over a cliff, they paused, hanging there, treading air, before gravity and the rush of air over wing surfaces took effect. The engine coughed. They were dropping. He saw a rainbow arch out of the gorge on the port side. He took it as a sign of hope. So did The Flier, banking towards it. The engine coughed again, then roared. The Flier struggled to gain control as they dived towards the gorge. There was another higher pitched engine scream behind them

*as the speedboat in pursuit sailed over the falls and its
propeller hit thin air. The poachers were still sitting in the
boat looking incuriously at them as their boat sailed down to
destruction in the gorge. The Flier lifted their nose and
narrowly missed a bridge in the mist as they climbed out of
the gorge to safety.*

*He looked over the side of the plane at the bushveld below.
He saw a herd of elephants, ears spread like sails, going in
formation like a fleet of grey galleons. The elephants were
saved.*

Flite Madison was Nick's greatest hero. He had
joined The Flier on many flights of imagination. A
green-painted bookshelf stood next to Nick's bed,
crammed with Flite Madison adventures. He chose a
book at random, opening it at the heart of the book
where the story was at its thickest, but instead of reading, he dipped his nose into the pages, breathing in its
familiar scent.

He loved to do that with his favourite books. He
loved the smell of them. With his nose almost touching
the converging line of print, he breathed in the odour of
paper and printer's ink, but to Nick the book did not
smell of these things. He detected a mixture of hot
metal, stale flying gear and the pungency of an aviation
engine at full throttle.

'The smell of a flying adventure,' he said to himself.
He could have picked it with his eyes closed. Each story
impregnated the pages with its own peculiar scent, Nick
believed. It was as individual as a signature. He let the
book fall onto his chest and crossed his arms over it. It
had a weight of memories beyond its real weight.

The Flier. The hero of his life.

Well, he wasn't entirely a hero. He had his dark side,

too. Yet he had been with Nick almost as long as he could remember, living in the wings of his life, not seen directly, merely glimpsed like a view seen from the corner of the eye.

We all needed heroes, Nick thought. Even the writer of his favourite books must have had his own storybook hero to inspire him. That was when Nick had the idea of writing an adventure story using his favourite character. He would call it 'Coming Down to Earth' and give it to Miss Ryder as the extra homework essay she had set for his punishment.

He would borrow The Flier for his story. It wouldn't be breaking the law, would it? He was only a fifteen-year-old boy writing an essay. He wouldn't be stealing, only borrowing. He wouldn't show anyone except Miss Ryder. He'd like to prove to her how well he could write, to show her how closely he had observed his favourite character. He would like to shine in her dark eyes. He wouldn't show his father. His father would laugh and call it copying. His father was a real writer of thriller stories.

Nick left the bed and, with the book under his arm, he went into his father's empty study. He sat down at a desk in front of his father's home computer, putting the Flite Madison adventure on top of the video monitor for inspiration. Then, with the smoothness of practice, he loaded the word processing program into the disk drive and tapped in a few key commands on the keyboard. The disk churned softly around inside the disk drive. It made a sound like digestion in progress.

Nick's eyes went to the illuminated screen where the cursor, a small white eye, started to wink insistently, urging him to begin. How much easier it must have been for the author of his favourite books. How much easier to write stories about The Flier than anyone *he* could possibly invent. The Flier performed expertly under his author's pen.

A flash of lightning went off like a snapshot taken outside the study window, throwing a quick shadow of his seated figure on a wall. Nick hesitated. Using the power was not a wise thing to be doing just then, a small voice in his mind warned him, but he went ahead anyway.

Using two fingers on the keyboard, he pecked out a name on the screen in capital letters: 'FLITE MADISON'. The name glowed there on the screen, a part of him, yet not his own. His eye travelled up to the Flite Madison adventure sitting on top of the square monitor.

He looked back at the screen. He straightened his spine in the chair. The chair was a little too comfortable and relaxing for a writer, he thought. Instead of keeping him alert, it lulled him.

Nick wrote for a bit, then stalled. Nothing happened for a long time. His eyes began to blink in time with the cursor on the screen. He closed his eyes to think, listened to the rain falling on the iron roof above him and, growing nearer, the tumble of thunder. Lightning flashed again. He saw the flare through his closed eyelids.

It was at that moment that the power momentarily died, shrinking the words on the screen into a single, hot, bright spot before they were sucked away into the great electronic unconsciousness.

When Nick opened his eyes, the room was dark and the computer screen was blank. The break only lasted for a few moments, then the screen flashed back to life, but the words were gone. The screen wore an empty look of surprise, like the look on his face.

He would have to start all over again. The rain eased off as he tried to recall what he had written. Soon the rain stopped. An urge came over him to go flying. He would have to try to fight it, even though the call was strong. You paid a price if you wanted to write adventure stories. You had to give up having adventures.

Nick wrote for a while, then broke off. His flight of imagination could wait for an hour or two while he enjoyed a real flying session, couldn't it?

Nick filed what he had written on a disk, then went back to his bedroom and took the float plane down off its line.

The S6B Supermarine float plane was a lean, propeller-driven racing machine with long, twin floats slung underneath its belly like torpedoes. It was the fastest thing in the air back in 1931 when it won the world's speed record for a float plane. But it was no match for an F14 jet.

He was flying his blue-and-white model float plane on a bare, scrubby stretch of the Encounter Coast near his home in South Australia when the Top Gun-style jet streaked from the shore and flicked across the sky above his float plane. It made a turn, its speed pushing it into a wide circle, before it came back over the shore. It was so realistic that he thought he was being buzzed by an Air Force pilot with a larrikin sense of humour. But it was a model, a ducted fan-jet that skimmed the air at 130 kilometres an hour. He looked around for its pilot. Was he hidden somewhere in the cliffs?

It took the F14 a long time to turn before it made another rush at his Supermarine. It passed so close this time it must have taken off the first layer of dope. The wash from its fan jet engine spun the Supermarine over on its back.

He straightened the Supermarine and took it coweringly low over the water, encouraging the jet to follow. It made another silvery, darting run, almost turning his plane over again. Then it was gone, turning for another run.

It was trying to force his float plane out to sea. Why? He could put down on water. The jet couldn't. It didn't make sense. He headed his plane for land. That would even things up a bit. There were cliffs to deal with there and a fan jet would take longer to react. It would give him a chance to employ some flying tactics and perhaps lure it into trouble.

He raced at a cliff. The jet followed. He went closer than he usually dared to go and then a bit closer before pulling back, using the updraught from the cliff face to help him over safely. The F14 did not fall for the trick. It pulled out of its run in plenty of time.

He wondered what damage the jet would do to his float plane if it hit him at 130 kilometres an hour. They would both turn into powder. Where was the pilot? He was getting tired of this game already. He had only recently had his float plane repaired at the hobby shop after its crackup.

The fan jet made another run at his float plane, shepherding him out to sea, then came back for another. His hands were getting moist on the controls.

Then he saw the boat out at sea, a cabin cruiser and a man standing in the stern and the flare of sunlight on a two-metre whip aerial. Somebody wanted to force his plane down into the sea, then recover it.

That gave him an idea. He turned the float plane's nose out to sea towards the cabin cruiser. He wanted to lure the jet into going above him, so he went into a climb. The jet followed, arrowing after his float plane like a missile. He pulled back on the throttle and let the float plane drop in a crippled Falling Leaf. The jet overshot him. He let the

Supermarine fall towards the sea. The jet turned to dive after him. Keep coming, he murmured. Keep coming. Just before he hit the water, he pulled out of it and made a landing on both floats and taxied tamely to the side of the cabin cruiser.

It threw the hijacker. He didn't know whether to try to make a grab for the plane or to concentrate on flying his fan jet. He decided to lean over the side of the boat and make a grab for the float plane with one hand. He went for a wingtip. The boy pressed a lever. The float plane turned on the man like a savage dog, its propeller buzz-sawing his outstretched hand. The man almost fell out of the boat as the boy gave his Supermarine some throttle and it sped away.

Forgotten, the abandoned F14 hit the sea and died with a whine like a squashed mosquito.

The boy turned the Supermarine into the wind and took off, flying her back towards the shore. The man on the cabin cruiser raised his arm and shook his fist in anger. The boy noticed he wasn't using the arm he had attacked; he was nursing it against his chest.

Why would somebody try to skyjack his model float plane? And why from a cabin cruiser out to sea? Were they trying to keep their identity a secret?

One day there was a surprise waiting for Nick at home. 'This arrived for you today,' his father said, handing him a bulky parcel wrapped in brown paper. Nick tore at a string tying it. The smell of new leather filled his nostrils even before he'd pulled the wrapping paper off. Leather glowed through the rips in the paper. Inside was a flying jacket, just like the flier's, in dark brown leather with zips and pockets in all the right places. It was exactly Nick's size, he soon discovered. He slipped it on in one fluid motion and ran the zip halfway up to his neck almost before the wrapping paper hit the floor. It was like jumping into another skin and into another self. The weight of brown leather held him, but also released him. Nick went up into the clouds. He swung his arms around and then bent them, scrunching the leather, making it creak in a most satisfying way. He guessed who had sent it.

He slipped a hand into one of the pockets and there he found his confirmation — a packet of stick gum, a small card that had greaseprints on it and a whiff of aviation fuel. The note said: 'From Big Flier to Little Flier. I like the way you fly, kid. Keep on taking risks.'

'I'm not the best father in the world, Nick,' his father said, looking puzzled, 'but I do know when it's your birthday and it isn't today. So what's going on? Who sent you the jacket?'

'A flying friend,' Nick said evasively, offering his father some gum and taking a stick of it himself. 'He flies real missions. He admires the way I fly.'

'That's quite an expensive jacket to give away. I hope his mother knows that he's parted with it.'

'I told you, he's a flier. He's a grown-up.'

Nick's father eyed the jacket dubiously. 'Not all that grown-up, apparently. His jacket fits you perfectly. What sort of aircraft does he fly — micro's?'

'This isn't *his* jacket, Dad. Maybe it's a spare jacket he found,' Nick said through a mouthful of tangy peppermint chewing gum. 'I don't know.' He shrugged his leather-covered shoulders. 'I'm not asking questions.'

'I am. You don't have the money to pay for a jacket like that. Tell me the truth, Nicholas. Did you swap something of yours to get it?'

'It's a gift. Don't you believe me?'

His father wanted to know more, but Nick just had to fly. Literally.

He went to his room to take his Supermarine float plane off its line so that he could go down to the cove.

'See you later, Dad.' He ran to the door.

'I won't be here when you get back. I'm going to Beth Ryder's for dinner,' Nick's father called after him. 'I'll leave a key under the potplant at the back door. There's some cold chicken in the refrigerator for your supper.'

Nick felt a reckless sense of adventure and freedom as he walked to his favourite flying spot. The jacket encouraged him to be daring. He skimmed the cliffs with his Supermarine and threw it around the sky in a series of daring rolls and spins.

3

The biplane

THE FLIER CAME ACROSS the cliff to join him.

'Skip school tomorrow and we'll go flying,' he said.

'I can't. I'd never get away with it. My father and my English teacher are friends.'

'Take a risk. You can make up a story.'

He was doubtful. 'How would I explain about going out of the door in the morning carrying my float plane?'

'You wouldn't have to. We're not using your plane. We're using my plane, a real one.'

'Can you fly with your injured hand?'

'Of course. A real plane's easier. You said so, remember? I don't need fingertip control like you do with radio-controlled model aircraft.'

He said goodbye to his father in the morning and went out of the door carrying his school case. When he was out of sight of the house he took his leather jacket out of the case and hid the case in some bushes. The flier was waiting around the corner. He gave him a welcoming wave with his bandaged hand. He was straddling a Harley Davidson motorcycle.

The flier handed him a spare helmet. 'Put that on. I like risks, kid, but not stupid ones.' The boy put on the helmet, ran the zip of his leather jacket under his chin and swung onto the back of the silver-and-black thunder-horse which roared away. The injured hand didn't stop the man riding a motor-cycle, he noticed. But then fingertip control wasn't a requirement for the way this man rode motorbikes. He was more interested in brute power and speed.

They took a side road and hammered along it into the country. The flier threw the big machine around corners and reared up along the straights. If this was the way his new friend flew at ground level, he could hardly wait to climb up in the clouds with him.

This was the way he wanted to feel. Screaming over the ground, the wind in his hair. The wind boiled around them and the earth blurred past.

The flier took them to a private airstrip. A few light aircraft stood outside a hangar. One caught his eye. It was a bright red vintage biplane with twin open cockpits and it looked eager to be airborne.

The flier parked the bike in the shade of the hangar and they took off their helmets. The boy's ears were still ringing from the clangour of the Harley.

'Can you fly a biplane?' he said.

'Kid, I can fly anything. Big planes, little planes, jet planes, paper planes. You name it, I fly it.'

'Are we going up in the biplane?' he said, hardly daring to hope.

'That's the plan.'

They went to it and he circled it reverently. A man in overalls came out from the hangar and had a word with the flier before going back to the hangar. He came back with a leather helmet and goggles for the boy who took them with a pretence of calmness and put on the helmet, fastening the chin strap. It was turning out to be quite a day. He added the *goggles to complete his transformation. He hoped he looked like an air ace. He probably looked more like Snoopy, he guessed. He had never flown in a real flying plane before, except commercial jets, but they weren't proper aeroplanes; they were computer-guided flying tubes. Biplanes were different. You really had to fly them.*

'Climb in,' the flier invited him. The man in overalls helped swing him up and he slid snugly into a small area that smelled wonderfully of aviation fuel and stale fabric and Flite Madison adventure books. 'Fasten the safety belt and parachute harness,' the flier called. 'You're a smart kid; you can work it out.'

Getting into the dark hole of the cockpit was like climbing into the innards of a piano. There were wires stretched over the wooden floorboards and the dark hole he sat in was trimmed with fabric and leather. Wires running tautly between the wings added to the impression of an instrument strung for play. There were even pedals. He moved them experimentally with his feet.

The biplane was evidently used as a trainer, the boy concluded. The cockpit was fitted with a complete set of dual controls. He compared the controls with the ones he was accustomed to on his model aeroplane, checking the collection of six instruments that sat on a dark painted panel before him. They weren't far removed from the ones he knew. The stumpy engine controls on the left weren't much bigger than the control levers on his radio transmitter. Pedals, a stick, instruments, a throttle. The same principles as his radio-controlled float plane, except these controls didn't hang on a box around his neck. It was probably less sophisticated than his Supermarine. It didn't even have a radio.

The windscreen, an oil-splattered wedge of glass, jutted above the cockpit. It hardly seemed necessary. He couldn't see through it because the biplane sat back on her haunches at a steep angle to the ground.

The mechanic helped the flier start her up. They gave her some shots of prime and swung the propeller through a few times.

After some hesitant coughs and kicks, she awoke. Mighty chords thundered in the flying piano and the cold stink of aviation fuel, laced with shreds of blue smoke, whipped over the boy.

The turmoil of a real propeller startled him. The giant twister seemed to threaten the safety of the entire structure. The wood and fabric trembled and the wires hummed. He threw a glance over his shoulder and saw the flash of a grin in the helmeted, goggled face of the flier.

The flier gave her throttle and the blazing fan of the propeller reached a new pitch, blowing an icy torrent over the cockpit. They were moving. He felt a tingle under his jacket. They trundled across the airstrip past a windsock on a pole. The flier turned them into the wind and made a bounding run at the sky. He took them up and at less than a hundred feet twisted in a roll that spun the boy's eyes around in their sockets like the button eyes in a toy golliwog.

He let out a whoop. It was half of joy and half of terror. It was so loud that the man at the controls must have heard him over the roar of the engine.

They went through aerobatic patterns, Outside Loops, Four Point Rolls and a Cuban Eight. These stunts were exciting enough for the boy when he was standing on the ground flying a model aeroplane operated by levers on a tiny box at his chest, but nothing had prepared him for the giddy thrill of sitting inside a real plane doing aerobatics. It was like taking a ride in an icy cold tumble drier except it didn't just go round and round; it had the ability to drop like an express lift to the ground where you risked having more than a mere crackup. You risked spreading yourself over a very large area of countryside.

Next the flier let the biplane drop, spiralling downwards in a Falling Leaf. The boy tensed for what seemed an age. He wondered quite analytically, separated from reality, just how big an area they would cover when they hit the ground. He didn't have to worry. The flier made a good recovery and took them up again. He wasn't going to try the boy's favourite stunt was he? He hoped not. He was nearing the edge of his nerve.

He remembered feeling that way once before when a friend had dared him to take a roller-coaster ride at a funfair. After the first loop, he knew he had made a terrible mistake. But there was no getting out of it. Then or now. Relax. Enjoy it. You may never have this chance again, he told himself.

The biplane climbed into a bright afternoon sky. The flier pulled out the throttle and the engine spluttered. Her powerplant seemed to die. Their momentum kept them climbing for a while before they paused, hanging. Then almost imperceptibly they began slipping back down their climbing track. The whole plane began to shriek and shudder in protest. It wasn't built to go backwards. The boy hoped that the flier wouldn't stall mentally the way he did when he attempted this trick. He threw a look over his shoulder. The flier hadn't frozen. He had gone to sleep, resting his head on his shoulder as if he were taking a Sunday afternoon nap.

They continued to fall.

The boy went hollow. 'Flier, are you okay?' he yelled. One stunt at a time was enough. Had he passed out? That awful feeling again. He had made a bad mistake. He should have gone to school. He'd be sitting safely in Miss Ryder's class right now, instead of backsliding into oblivion.

But it was only the flier's little joke.

The pilot gave the boy a teasing grin and then snapped out of it. The aircraft gave a shudder. The engine lifted in pitch, but by then they were in a spin and he watched powerlessly, trusting in the flier's skill. He recovered well. He came out of a Tail Slide with a lot more dignity than the boy did.

The flier set them on a level course back towards the airfield.

It had been fun, but he was damp with sweat. He loved flying, but he could only stand so much excitement. He was thankful it was coming to an end, he had to admit.

It wasn't.

He turned to give the flier a grateful wave of thanks and was horrified to see the man clambering out of the cockpit onto the wire-strutted wing. The man groped along it towards the boy, the wind fattening his cheeks. Leaning his face as close as he could to the boy he yelled, 'Remember what you said about flying models? You said it was harder than flying a real aeroplane. Now's your chance to prove it. See you on the ground.'

'Are you mad?' the boy shrieked. 'I'm just a kid.'

'You're a flier. Now be a real one. Think of all those books you've read. Think of all those flying hours you've had. . . take a few risks. . .'

He stepped out into the sky and dropped away like a stone.

It was the loneliest moment of the boy's life.

He twisted around, hoping to find that it was another joke and that the man was clinging to the tail or something. He wasn't. He craned over the side of the cockpit and he saw a stream of bright silk ribboning out behind the falling man like blood streaming from a cut under water, then the parachute spouted open and checked his fall. He was on target for the airstrip.

The boy shrank inside the cockpit to hide. He stayed that way for a while with his head stuck into his leather jacket like a turtle in its shell. Maybe when he came out it would all be over.

This was the way he wanted to feel, wasn't it? Screaming over the sky, the wind howling around him? Yes, but not alone, not up here.

He was just a school kid.

He groped for some explanation. Maybe this was a radio-controlled plane that could be operated from the ground. Maybe the plane was already in the grip of a transmitter held in the flier's strong hands and there was nothing at all to worry about.

He glanced at the altimeter dial and knew it wasn't true. His fear was confirmed by a glimpse of the horizon which had suddenly tilted crazily. He was going into a dive.

Should he reach for the stick? Once he did, once he touched it, he would be accepting control of the plane. He wanted to postpone that moment, wanted somebody — anybody — to take over. He remembered hearing stories of absolute beginners being talked down to the ground by a calm voice in a control tower. Was that it? The flier was going to tell him what to do, to help him land this thing step by step. He had nothing to worry about. Any moment now a radio would crackle blessedly into life and he would hear the flier's voice and calm instructions. No, that couldn't be true. No voice would be coming along to ease his fears. There was no radio in this old barnstormer. But surely the man wouldn't just leave him to it? He wasn't that reckless. He remembered the flier's words on the Harley Davidson when he had given him a helmet to wear: 'I like risks, kid, but not stupid ones.' What greater risk could he take than this one? It didn't make sense.

Maybe it was something else. Maybe the flier believed the boy could actually fly it if he tried. Maybe he had simply overestimated his level of ability. It was the price he was paying for showing off. Stupid kid, acting like some big time air ace. He was just a toy plane flier. Dressing up in a leather flying jacket and wearing a helmet and goggles couldn't change that.

His father and Miss Ryder would never know what had happened to him. Nor would Kate. 'How had a kid who flew model aeroplanes wiped himself out in a vintage biplane?' everybody would ask.

It wasn't a pleasant feeling to be granted all that you wished for in life, the boy thought. He had adventure now. He had excitement. He had fear running in cold rivers down the inside of his new jacket.

He had no trouble seeing through the oil-smeared windshield. At the angle of his dive he could look over the nose and see the ground rushing to meet him. He couldn't put off the decision for ever. He had to try. Hesitantly, he took the stick in his hand and pulled back. Miracles. It happened. The biplane's nose lifted. Simple as that.

Miracles. Joy.

She answered. They levelled out.

A simple tug on a stick. It was the most important flying manoeuvre he had ever made. The boy allowed himself the luxury of wallowing for a while in his success, at least while the sweat dried under his jacket. He steadied her on a level course and flew towards the horizon, but he was getting further and further away from the airfield. He would have to risk a turn. Manoeuvre number two. He was pushing it. He decided to bank to the port side and he kicked the port pedal. He turned. Left was left and right was right. Instinctive. Not like a radio-controlled model. When a model flew *towards you, things were much more complicated.*

He fed in some trim and straightened. This might not be total disaster after all. But he had better get downstairs. He eased back on the throttle and took the biplane down in a shallow descent towards the airstrip.

He came in slowly. Up ahead he made out the figure of the flier sitting on an oil drum looking up at the sky. He had taken off his helmet and goggles and he waved them in one hand.

'Good boy,' he was probably thinking. 'Knew you could do it, kid.' His gamble with a boy and a frail old aeroplane had paid off. The boy saw him laugh.

That did it. He decided to fly the smile right off that upturned face. He veered towards the flier and passed so low overhead that he tipped him off his oildrum. The drum went over with the fallen flier and rolled right over his head.

Now the boy laughed a bit in a cracked kind of way.

It was his turn to play. He wasn't stupid enough to try a tail slide, but a victory roll worked well enough and so did an inside loop, although he didn't come out of it with much air to spare and the flier was clutching the top of his head by the time he pulled out of it.

He might just take the biplane to Cuba. No, that was too far. How about Kangaroo Island? No good either. Air officials might have something to say about a school kid taxiing in to Kingscote Airport.

He decided to put the flier out of his misery and turned around. He made another approach. It wasn't exactly a 3-in-1 'oil-can landing' as the pros called it, but it was smooth enough for a boy who flew toy aeroplanes.

He cut the throttle. He managed to hide his shakiness as he clambered down and swaggered across the strip.

'You've earned your wings, kid. I hope it proves something

to you. You never know what you can do until you try.'

The boy supposed that hero-types like the flier had to behave in that reckless way.

If they weren't being daring, they wouldn't be interesting. Yet it made them predictable in a way.

4

Beth Ryder

HIS ENGLISH TEACHER, MISS RYDER, hesitated before handing back Nick's latest essay, taking off a pair of reading glasses to look at him with puzzled dark eyes.

'Your piece "Coming Down to Earth" was quite a surprise, Nick. I'd like the rest of the class to hear it.'

Miss Ryder read it out to the class. She read it with all the right emphasis. He felt himself glowing with pleasure. When she had finished, Kate, the red-headed girl in the desk next to Nick's, shook her head and sighed — probably in admiration, he guessed. Nick paid everyone the compliment of thinking they were admirers.

'I've given your flying story a high grade,' Miss Ryder concluded, 'and I've added this comment: "Highly original — almost ninety-nine per cent original Flite Madison."'

Nick coloured even more with pleasure.

'Thanks.'

'Don't thank me. Thank the ghost of the original author who haunts your story. Why don't you simply call your hero Flite Madison and be done with it? Next time, please hand in your *own* assignments.'

Miss Ryder didn't mean it as praise, he saw now. He felt the classroom turn around him. Miss Ryder's dark eyes lost their puzzlement and filled with concern for him. 'Nick, you show in this story that you have everything an imagination needs to create thrilling stories. You have an engaging style and a mind stocked with vivid, glowing characters, characters with whom we can all instantly identify. There's only one problem. The style you are using and the characters who people your brain are not your own. They belong between the covers of your favourite books. I know you admire other writers, but you really shouldn't steal their creations.'

'I only borrowed them,' he said in a defensive voice, feeling hurt. 'I didn't steal.'

He caught the eye of the girl in the desk next to his. Cool-eyed Kate gave him a smile. It was a typical Kate smile. Superior. Yet he imagined he saw some sympathy there. The bell sounded for the next period.

In a lowered voice, Miss Ryder said gently: 'Stay behind a moment, Nick. I'd like a word with you.'

He shrugged indifferently. The others got up from their desks to go. Kate gave him another smile before she left the classroom with the others. It confirmed Nick's suspicion. There was a hint of sympathy there. She was on his side. She was probably jealous of Miss Ryder. All the girls were. They copied the way she fixed her dark hair, fringed at the front and falling in a waterfall around her face like a noblewoman in an ancient Egyptian fresco. They had all stopped wearing pony tails. The fringe and waterfall looked particularly fine on Kate with her sunset-red hair.

After the lesson, alone with Nick in the empty classroom, Miss Ryder slid behind a desk — Kate's desk — next to his. It was both a strange and a delightful sight to see Miss Ryder sitting behind a pupil's desk. He found it an admirable thing to do. He found most things admirable about Miss Ryder, including the way she dressed. Today she looked very pure and summery in a cool white cotton dress. Miss Ryder cleared her throat, then put on reading glasses defensively. He was glad she did that. She was not so pretty with the glasses on and a little easier to face.

'This is not something I welcome saying. You're not going to like it. And I find it particularly hard to say to you of all people, since your father is a writer. Have you ever thought, Nick, that perhaps your gift is for reading?'

'That's not a gift.'

'Oh yes it is. It's a great gift. We can't all be transmitters, the ones who create. Some must be receivers, the ones who appreciate — and some receivers are more finely attuned than others. A wise man called Jung once said that in a sense even God needs an audience — that we are like his nerve endings that allow him to experience himself and his creation. He wondered what God would do if the applause for creation suddenly stopped and everybody stopped appreciating. We can't all create. Somebody has to be the reader, the viewer, the one in the dark of the theatre or movie house who vibrates like a musical instrument to the playing. You should read, not write, I believe, particularly at your age. You are a perfect, loving reader and creation can't afford to lose you.'

'But I want to write.'

'Read, at your age,' she said, imploringly. 'You're a born reader. It shows in your writing how deeply you love what you read. Some people merely read, but you do more. You pass into what you read as if you were a liquid and the page were a permeable membrane. You become absorbed in it. You are every author's dream reader because you appreciate so deeply. You are the reason why authors write.'

'I'm going to be a writer,' Nick said stubbornly. 'You'll see.'

He rose to leave.

'Please sit down.'

He sank back into his chair, squirming.

'You needn't glare at me like that, Nick. Please understand that I have your best interests at heart. I'm not your enemy. I'm your English teacher and a friend, a personal friend of the family. Your friend as much as your father's. And it's no secret to say that I'm going to become something more to you and your father. . .'

He avoided her eye. He knew what she meant. It made his insides tremble, partly in misgiving and partly in pleasure, for he could be melted by a look from the darkly mysterious Miss Ryder even though he couldn't bear to listen to what she was saying. It was a bit of a shock when your pretty English teacher and your father planned to marry, especially when you loved to write essays to impress her and she, disloyally, preferred your father's writing to your essays just because he was a published author and you were only a fifteen-year-old.

'You really ought to stop trying to be a storyteller, Nick. It's not convincing because you haven't lived life yet.'

'I can write just as well as my father.'

She gave him a sad look. 'You can't compare yourself with your father. Your father has lived, travelled the world to gain experiences and material for his books. Stick to writing what you know about. Write factual essays instead.'

'I can write great stories,' he said with a dull conviction that felt like a deep-seated ache in his stomach. 'I won't ever stop.'

'Lawrence tells me you spend a lot of your time writing,' she went on. 'A boy your age should be out enjoying life, appreciating things, living deeply and reading widely, stocking his mind for the future. Live life a bit, Nick, enjoy it. See how you feel about writing when you're a little older. Please listen to what I'm saying. Will you think about what I said?'

'Fine, Miss Ryder,' he said. But he had already made up his mind not to obey her. What she was saying was too painful to hear.

What she was saying was enough to drive him back to the word processor, more determined than ever. He did not want to do what she said. He wanted to do exactly the opposite. He wanted to give up reading forever.

'You'll have to stop calling me Miss Ryder when we're together,' she said in a softened voice. 'I'm Beth.'

Beth. He could call her Beth.

It almost made up for the shock of what she had said. Almost, but not quite.

If that's what Miss Ryder thinks of my writing, I'll show her, he thought. I'll stop being the world's best reader. I'll never read a book again, not unless I have to. From now on I'll dedicate myself to writing. I'll write something that will convince her that I was born to write, not read, and I will make her admire me for it. I will never read again until then, he vowed.

Nick's vow about reading was soon put to the test. The next day they had a library period at school. He wandered up and down the rows of bookshelves in the school library, pretending to look for a book, but allowing the book titles to slide by in an unfocussed haze.

'Looking for a story to borrow, Nick? Or to steal like you did with your essay?'

'Not you, too!'

Kate. She was at the end of a bookshelf, wearing her superior smile. During a reading period in the school library they were supposed to choose a book and sit reading at one of the reading tables.

'Why did Miss Ryder ask you to stay back yesterday?'

'She thinks I should stop writing. She says I'm too young to be spending my time writing stories. That I should live life first. And stick to reading.'

'Perhaps she's trying to give you some good motherly advice.' Kate said the word 'mother' in a loaded way.

'She's not my mother.'

'Yet.'

Kate knew. They all knew. 'What are you going to do?' she said.

'I'm not going to listen to her, if that's what you mean. In fact, I'm going to stop reading books ever again. I'm going to concentrate on being a writer.'

'Is that wise? You'll never pass exams that way.'

'Then I'll only read what I have to read.'

The bookish Kate already had a book under one arm

and was looking for another. 'I always thought you were sensible, because you liked to read,' she said with a small frown. 'Stopping reading would be a very silly thing to do.'

'You liked my story, didn't you, Kate? What makes her think I don't know anything about life yet? I'm writing about what I know, about things I've experienced.'

Her blue eyes locked Nick in a narrow gaze.

'I liked it. But who was writing it? You?'

'Of course it was me.'

'Or your favourite author?'

'Me.'

'She was a bit rough on you,' Kate said, conceding the fact in a gentler tone. 'Don't take it too hard, though. I think she's tougher on you than she is on the rest of us. She wants to show everybody that there's no favouritism.'

The others in the class were sitting down at the library reading tables reading their books. Kate and Nick were the only two left standing. The school librarian noticed them. The stooped, skinny Miss Henshaw came pacing between the bookshelves, like a stalking egret wading in the shallows ready to pounce on frogs and insects and boys who took too long choosing books.

'Come along. Don't stand there propping up the shelves,' Miss Henshaw said briskly.

'Pick a book,' Kate whispered, prodding him.

'I told you, I'm not going to read any more.'

'Then pretend.'

Miss Henshaw came close, arching over him, ready to peck. Nick pulled a book at random from the shelf and followed Kate to one of the reading tables.

They sat down. Kate put her books on the table, and Nick mechanically did the same. He noticed the title of the book in front of him. He groaned inwardly. It was a Judy Blume paperback. He had mistakenly picked up a girl's book. The paperback was titled: *Are You There, God? It's Me, Margaret.*

'Don't you dare!' Kate said in a blazing whisper, noticing his book.

'What?'

'Rip off Judy Blume!'

'I'm not. I just picked it up at random. Do you think I'd steal a girl's story?'

Miss Henshaw, who had the hearing of a night owl, did not miss the whispered exchange. She had also noticed with interest which book he had chosen off the shelf. She came to Nick and stooped over him in her bird-like manner. 'Please let the class see what you are reading, Nick. Hold it up.'

Colouring, he held up the book.

'Judy Blume,' she said, and then she read out the title in a very loud voice for a librarian. '*Are You There, God? It's Me, Margaret.* Good for you, Nick. I'm glad to see the barriers are finally coming down in our school library. There should be more of it. I never did believe in girls' books and boys' books.'

She went off, making a clucking sound in her throat which in Miss Henshaw signified amusement.

The boys in the class looked at Nick in pity, the girls with new respect. He shuddered. The girls suddenly think I'm a caring and sensitive male, he thought. How would he live it down? Kate had no such illusions. She viewed him with suspicion. 'Leave Judy Blume alone.'

'I will, I will,' he whispered.

What you picked up to read, even by accident, could get you into a lot of trouble, he was beginning to discover. Miss Henshaw sat at her desk and trained her gaze on him. Did she really expect him to read it?

Nick lifted the book, opened it and was about to dip his nose into its heart to subject it to his customary sniff test when he checked himself, looking guiltily around to see if the boys were still watching. They weren't, but a few of the girls were, a fact which Kate had not failed to notice. Nick looked at the book and secretly sniffed once or twice. Even at arm's length, he could smell its peculiar scent. A girl's book smell, nothing like an adventure story. The slender paperback book in his hands had the forbidden scent of a girl's bedroom or handbag, places that boys were discouraged from entering. Nick turned to the blurb on the back of the book. It said: 'I just told my mother I wanted a bra. Please help me grow, God. You know where. . .'

He coloured a little more.

Quickly, he flipped the book over, opening to the front page. He stared as if reading, but without seeing, the first page.

'Waiting for the wind to turn your page, Nicholas Young?' Miss Henshaw called out tartly from the counter at the front where she sat on a stool. 'I'll open a window if you like.'

He turned the page with apparent interest, but he was taking in nothing. The lines danced in front of his angry stare. If he was never going to read his favourite books again, he certainly wasn't going to read this one. He turned to the next page, and then to the next.

'You see, girls' books aren't that bad,' Kate whispered.

'I hoped you wouldn't find out. Now Judy Blume is in trouble.'

After the reading period, Kate walked beside Nick across a concrete netball area to their next class, a temporary prefabricated building. She seemed to have guessed what else Miss Ryder had said to him.

'Is she going to marry your dad?' Kate said shrewdly.

He shrugged. 'What do I care?'

'You care all right. I see the way your ears go red when she talks to you. All you boys are the same with Miss Ryder. And now you must face having her in the same house with you and your father every single day. Taking over your kitchen. Doing her laundry with yours.'

Nick felt his eyes widen momentarily at the prospect. 'No, I don't think that'll happen. My dad's pretty good in the kitchen and cooks all our meals. And I usually do my own laundry. I don't see why things would change.'

'They will,' she promised him. 'Everything will change. She'll redecorate. She'll leave her cosmetics around in your bathroom and her shampoos and conditioners will pile up on the shelf in your shower. She'll sit across from you at the breakfast table every morning when you're looking your groggiest. And think of this. There'll be no more getting out of doing your homework and no excuses for missing school. You can't ask Miss Ryder to write notes for you. It's going to be as if school's started from the moment you open your eyes in the morning. It's going to be very confusing for a boy like you and you're going to need help. I just wanted to tell you that I understand and that you can always talk to me,' Kate said, in a sympathetic, yet superior Kate way.

He imagined Miss Ryder sitting at their sunny breakfast table every morning, standing at their yellow kitchen counter, sharing their bathroom shower that always managed to squirt water over the floor no matter how careful you were. Nick had often tried to imagine Miss Ryder living with them before, but he'd only seen it through a mist as if he were trying to view a scene through a steamed-up window, but now, invoked mischievously by Kate, the picture cleared and the full, squirming reality of it pressed against him. He pictured Miss Ryder standing in the bathroom doorway dressed in a bathrobe and her hair in curlers and he saw himself stumbling down the corridor to the bathroom, bleary-eyed and dressed only in boxer shorts. He heard Miss Ryder give a chuckle at the sight of his gangly legs. He went hot, both in the scene and in reality.

'Why are you blushing, Nick?' Kate said.

'Just thinking of what it's going to be like.'

Kate was a comfort.

Nick awoke early the next morning to write on his father's word processor. He had scarcely loaded the program and begun to tap away at the keys when his father came into the study, tying a knot in the belt of his white dressing gown.

'Hi, Dad.'

'Your writing habits are putting me to shame, Nick,' his father said. He checked his wristwatch, blinking sleepily. 'Five-thirty in the morning and you've already made a start.'

'I have to use the processor early. You use it at night.'

'Complaining now, are you? You'd like it at night, too? You make me feel like a dabbler and I'm supposed to be the professional writer. I suppose you've never heard of writer's block,' he said in a complaining way. His father loved to adopt a mock-complaining tone as if his life as a writer were embattled by circumstance.

'Early mornings are the only time I can be sure of getting it.'

'I'm sorry to hog it at night, Nick. I must be playing havoc with your creative flow. But try to understand, my publisher is less reasonable than your English teacher.'

'I don't know about that.'

A look of recollection passed like a frown over his youthful face. 'Oh yes, I remember.' He ran a hand tiredly through his wavy blond hair. 'Beth told me about your story. If it's any consolation, she rips my work to shreds, too. She can be pretty tough. Do you know that she laughs at my spelling?' He pulled up a chair next to Nick's. 'I'd like to swap literary notes with you, Nick, but not now. I'm here to discuss a small housekeeping matter. I want to talk to you about Beth.'

'You don't have to tell me about Beth. I know what you're going to say.'

'You need a mother.'

'No, I don't,' Nick said firmly.

'Then you need help with your essays. She's very good. With Beth around you're bound to get higher marks. What mark did she give you for your last effort?'

'Seventeen out of twenty.'

'Seventeen out of twenty!' He whistled. 'That's better than a Booker prize. Your literary efforts are crowned with success. She gave my last manuscript a caning.'

'Why are you doing it, Dad?'

'It's my spelling,' his father said in a confessional tone. 'I need help. Having Beth here would be like having a live-in dictionary, or a spell-check program on my word processor. She's great. You may have noticed that I don't bother to print out my work any more. I just leave my stuff on the disk and when Beth comes round, she loads it up, reads it and corrects my spelling and grammar before the publisher ever sees it. She reads anything I leave around.'

'I've noticed.'

'She'd do the same with your essays. She'd give you a mark before you left for school.'

His father said things in a grave-sounding voice, totally out of place with the playful twist of his words.

'Be serious, Dad.'

'That's the trouble with your generation. Too serious. Your generation wouldn't think of dropping out of society to write books. You have to stay plugged in. . . to word processors.'

'You're going to marry her,' Nick said in a dead voice. 'Yes.'

'And she's going to come and live here with us and leave her cosmetics and shampoos and conditioners in our bathroom and sit with us every mealtime, even breakfast.'

'That's generally what happens when you marry a woman. I could ask Beth to take her showers some-where else and eat all her meals out, but wives aren't that flexible.'

'My teacher will suddenly turn into my stepmother,'

he said in dread, as if contemplating a horror scene.

'You make it sound like Dracula's bride transforming into a bloodsucking creature. She's a lovely lady. I'm not doing this to make your life awkward, Nick. I'm fond of her. No — let me say it — I love her.'

'I don't know about this,' Nick said dubiously.

'Please don't refuse me. At least think about it. I couldn't stand an outright No from my son,' he said playfully.

'I suppose I can't stop you.'

'Not really, I'm a grown man.'

'And it's your life.'

'You're very wise, son, because if you didn't agree we'd just run away and get married anyway. You know what adults are like. We're getting married next week, by the way, then we're going on honeymoon to Kangaroo Island.'

'You can't.'

'Why not?'

'That's where you and I have our holidays together,' Nick said in protest.

'Exactly. And you'll be coming, too,' his father said, surprising him.

'On your honeymoon?'

'Not quite. You'll be following us later, after a week or so. We want a bit of time alone so we can get used to each other's shampoos and conditioners, that sort of thing. Then when we've sorted out the details, it's time for you to join us for the Christmas holidays. You'll come over with Popper.'

'Popper's coming here?' Popper was Nick's grandfather, only he hated being called grandfather.

'I didn't tell you. You'll be babysitting Popper while

we're away. Then we'll all meet up for a jolly family holiday on the island.'

'I see.'

'I'm afraid there's another bombshell to come, Nick. It's about the word processor. I'm taking it with me to the island. I've got to squeeze in a bit of writing in between honeymooning. My next book's overdue.'

'But I can't write without a word processor.'

'Welcome to writer's block, son.' His father patted him on the back. 'Have you ever tried writing in an exercise book? A lot of schoolboys start that way.'

How could his father be so inconsiderate?

'No more congratulations, please,' his father said in a protesting voice. 'I can't sit here shaking your hand and being patted on the back. I'll cook us some breakfast.'

'There's just one thing I'd like to ask,' Nick said. 'May I bring a friend to the island?'

'I suppose so. Who?'

'Kate,' he said, inexplicably.

'You want to take a girl?'

'You're taking one.'

His father shrugged. 'I suppose I am. Kate's parents can hardly object. She'll have a schoolteacher keeping an eye on her. And speaking of schoolteachers, I've invited Beth to join us for dinner one night this week. I thought you two could start getting used to having each other around.'

Nick felt a tremor in his stomach. 'You don't have to do this.'

'I know, but I'd like to,' he said. 'You will be pleasant, won't you? Promise you won't be a surly resentful boy!' he said teasingly.

Nick went back to his writing.

He did not know how to face Miss Ryder at school that day. Every time he stole a glance at her long black hair, shining in the light of the window near her desk, he kept thinking of her bottles of shampoo and conditioner piling up in their shower at home.

Kate noticed the change in him. 'Come and tell me all about it,' she said at break time. He did. 'Poor Nick,' she said, sadly. But she brightened when he invited her to the island.

5

The wedding

HE WENT FLYING after school the next day. Carrying his model float plane, he went down some rocks to the cobalt blue waters of a sheltered cove. He crouched over the float plane and ran through some checks. Then he stood back, the transmitter on a harness at his chest, and he operated the knobs and switches, each movement producing a visible response on a control surface of the aeroplane as the pulse set one tiny actuator after another in operation. Everything was functioning smoothly.

Nick started up the float plane's engine, running it across the calm waters of the cove and into the wind, leaving a small, spreading wake like a smile on the surface, a tiny plume of smoke issuing from its engine. Using the radio controls, he gave it throttle, fed in some elevator and lifted the little aeroplane off the water in a slow, realistic take-off before heading up into a leaden sky.

There was a man standing near a parked car at the roadside watching him through a pair of binoculars. Nick felt like trying a few stunts, so he put the aircraft through a series of loops, rolls and spins, ending off with a Tail Slide that made his own hands damp. The usual thing happened. He went into one of his mental stalls. He just snapped out of it in time.

He took the float plane in a wide circle over the water and brought it down.

The man came over from the roadside.

'Nice plane,' he said. 'I'd like to buy it.'

'Why?' the boy said.

He didn't look like a radio-control enthusiast. He looked more like a headmaster. He was a tall, beaky man with puffs of hair on the sides of his tweed cap.

'I like the way it handles. Sell it to me and I'll give you enough money to buy yourself the best model aircraft money can buy.'

'I don't want another aircraft.'

'What do you want? You must want something.'

'A word processor.'

'You can't do much flying with that — unless you prefer flights of imagination.'

'I like both. How much are you offering?'

'A thousand dollars for the plane and a thousand dollars for you if you fly it for me.'

'You want it pretty badly. Why do you want me to fly it for you?'

'I can't fly.'

'Where's the fun in watching me fly an aeroplane for you?'

'It isn't a joy flight. I want you to fly it somewhere on a mission,' he said. 'It'd be a real test of your flying ability, a tricky bit of flying. At night.'

'Where do you want me to fly?'

'Out to sea,' he said. 'It's top secret, a sort of test of our defences shall we say. Will you do it?'

Two thousand dollars. It would allow the boy to buy a word processor of his own. And a disk drive.

'Two thousand,' he said again. 'But say a word about this to anybody and it's all off. Secrecy, remember. Will you do it?' The boy looked up into the pink, beaky face under the tweed cap.

'Maybe I will, maybe I won't,' he said. 'It depends.'

'Depends on what?'

'On when it is. I won't be here for much longer. I'm going to Kangaroo Island soon.'

The man was surprised. He scowled a bit, but he wasn't deterred. 'Kangaroo Island changes things a bit, but no matter: it will do. Perhaps it will do even better, come to think of it.'

'Then we'll see.'

'I'll contact you on Kangaroo Island.'

'Who are you?' he said.

'I'm a sort of scientist. You can call me doctor.'

'Doctor what?'

'Who,' the man corrected him in a headmasterish tone.

'You're Doctor Who?'

'No.'

'Doctor No.'

'Just doctor.'

'How about just Doc?'

The man rolled his eyes despairingly. He looked more like a headmaster than a scientist. The boy had seen him before. He was the man who had come into the Hobby Hangar shop. The boy wondered if he was the man who had tried to hijack his plane.

Why was everyone suddenly taking such an interest in his model float plane?

The boy dreamt of flying his Supermarine out to sea that

night. He saw the mysterious silhouette of a vessel lying in
near darkness in the water lit only by a sliver of moon. He
was standing near a white lighthouse, overlooking a cliff.
Waves broke on jagged rocks below him. He saw the flier
standing beside him in the moonlight and he saw the glint of
his teeth as he gave him an encouraging smile.

'Do it, kid,' he said. 'Show them.'

His father was out with Beth, so Nick went into his
bedroom to think.

A man dressed in flying gear lounged on his bed. The boy
almost dropped his float plane. He twisted, holding the float
plane in front of him like a shield.

'How did you get in here?'

'Good friends don't have to announce themselves,' the flier
said. He had the look of a Battle of Britain pilot trying to
relax while he waited for orders to scramble.

The boy wondered how he had found the key to the house.
Had he seen his father put it under the potplant?

'Did you meet my father?'

'Are you kidding? I don't think your father should know
about me. Nor should anybody else,' he said.

'Why?'

'I don't like drawing attention.'

'Then why did you send me this jacket? My father was
full of questions.'

'What did you tell him?'

'The truth. That a real flier gave it to me. He didn't
believe a word of it.'

'Then relax,' he said. 'Do you like it?'

'Like it?' the boy said. 'It's an amazing jacket. I don't
know how to thank you.'

'You look like the real thing,' he said. 'And now you have a real mission.'

The boy tied his float plane to wires from the ceiling, giving it a push so that it slowly circled above them.

'How do you know?'

'I was watching you today. I've often watched you. That man today hired you for a mission. Am I right?'

'If you know so much, tell me why they want my plane and why they want me to fly it.'

'I can't say.'

'There's nothing on my plane,' the boy said. 'I've checked it thoroughly. Unless. . .'

'Unless what?'

The turning plane threw shadows over the wall. A memory flitted across the boy's mind like one of the shadows. He scratched in a cupboard where he turned up a scrapbook. It was his model aeroplane scrapbook. He opened it, turning up a yellowing newspaper cutting.

'What have you found?' the flier said.

'It's a story that first appeared in an English newspaper. I'll read it to you:

'Mini planes fly in deadly cargo

'Smuggling is alive and well — in fact flourishing — on the coast of Cornwall, but the contraband and the methods have changed. Once it was brandy run ashore in a longboat. Today it is a deadly cargo of drugs flown in by radio-controlled aircraft.

'A flight of fantasy?

'No, say the Customs men who are out to get the culprits.

'A mysterious discovery was made recently when fishermen reported sighting the wreckage of an aircraft in the sea off Fowey. Closer investigation by the authorities who recovered the wreckage revealed it to be the remains of a sophisticated model aircraft. Although no cargo was found on board, a hidden compartment was found in the model's fuselage.

'"We were able to work out the dimensions of the aircraft from the bits," a Customs spokesman said today. "It is clearly no toy, with a wingspan of around six feet and an all-up weight of over twelve pounds. That in itself would make the aircraft illegal," he said, "since Air Navigation Orders strictly limit the maximum weight of models to eleven pounds and it would have to have a special licence to fly."

'The aircraft is reported to have been equipped with a sophisticated radio receiver, a fuel-driven silenced engine and a retractable undercarriage complete with pneumatic tyres. All in all a sophisticated tool in the hands of modern-day smugglers.

'The discovery came as a culmination of a series of perplexing clues, reports of flashing lights offshore and strange signals picked up on a frequency outside the set frequency band designed by the Post Office for radio control hobbyists.

'It is believed that models with a capacity of up to three kilograms are being launched from darkened cabin cruisers offshore and flown by an operator on land to a pick-up spot behind the coast. From there the deadly cargo is taken to London where it fetches a fortune on Britain's lucrative drug trade.

'Police and Customs officials are still investigating this bizarre new twist on an age old Cornish pursuit.'

'This is your break, kid. What a great test of your flying

skills, flying a model plane out to a ship at night! I wonder what will be out there waiting on the water? A darkened cabin cruiser? Or the black silhouette of a submarine lying low and deadly in the water?'

'Don't you understand? They plan to put dope on my plane.'

'Dope. I haven't heard that word used in years.'

'Don't you care what they're doing?'

'I doubt if it's drugs. But I wouldn't get too nosy. As long as the money is good, fly it. The more mysterious the flight, the better. Think of the challenge. You've been hired for your flying skills, so use them.'

'Don't you have morals?'

'Morals are for sermons. This is an adventure. You've got the chance to enjoy some real action. Don't you want experience, kid?'

Experience. That was what Beth Ryder said he lacked. That was what was missing from his writing.

He was surprised by the flier's cynical attitude, yet excited by the challenge of the flying. 'You don't care about the cargo?'

The flier snapped his fingers. 'Not that much. There's only one question: are you up to it or not? Simple as that. Do you think you can pull off a flight to a waiting ship in the dark?'

'I can do it,' the boy said.

'Good. Just keep thinking of the money.'

The boy supposed that action was the most important thing in a flying hero's life. He shouldn't be surprised by his reaction, he told himself. The flier probably accepted mysterious missions every day. And he was right. It would be exciting.

Beth arrived for dinner dressed casually in faded denim jeans and a shirt, a contrast to her glossy dark hair. She smiled at Nick brightly, walking arm-in-arm with his father into the lounge.

'Hi there,' Nick said, without getting up. He was slouched on a chair in the lounge, hunched in his leather jacket, swinging a leg idly over the arm of a chair and chewing lazily on a stick of gum, like a fighter pilot waiting for a call to scramble.

'Hello Nick,' she said. 'Love your jacket. You almost look like a real flier.'

'I am a real flier,' he said. 'I can fly real planes.'

Beth and his father exchanged looks. 'You have quite an imagination, Nick,' Beth said, making it sound like a criticism.

'I should hope so. I'm a writer. Where would I be without one?'

'I'm afraid Nick has the vivid imagination in this house,' his father said, inviting Beth to take a seat.

'Something's burning in the kitchen, Larry,' Beth said with a smile. It was a hint to get rid of him. She wanted to have a word with Nick in private.

His father gave her a wink of complicity and went to the kitchen to finish a dish of spaghetti bolognaise that he was preparing for their dinner.

'I noticed you missed school,' she said when his father was safely out of earshot in the kitchen. 'Do you want to tell me why?'

'I was flying a vintage biplane, a real one, doing aerobatic stunts on my own.'

'I see. You don't want to tell me. Well, don't worry, I haven't told your father.'

He shrugged indifferently. 'Do what you like.'

'Is something wrong, Nick? You're not upset about your father and me, are you?'

'Why should I be? If that's what you and Dad want to do, that's up to you. I've got my own stuff to think about.'

'I'm glad. I'd hate to feel I was causing a problem for you.'

If only you knew, he thought.

There was more force in his gaze than he wanted to show. She flinched and looked away.

He picked up a remote control switch for the television and flicked up and down the channels annoyingly to prevent her from questioning him further. He turned up the volume. It worked. Beth got up and went to help his father in the kitchen. He felt a tiny bit guilty. He wished he didn't like Beth Ryder.

Nick's father was a good cook and his spaghetti was Nick's favourite. Beth was full of approval, too. Nick felt himself relaxing in her company. She was only a visitor after all. She didn't live here. Yet.

There was something on Nick's mind.

'You're a writer, Dad,' he said, twirling some strands of spaghetti around his fork.

'Thankyou, Nick. I feel elevated to a new status. That's the first time you've ever conferred that title on me.'

'It's about heroes. What is it about them?' Nick said. Beth stopped eating to listen. Something about his tone attracted her attention. 'Why are they so heartless?' he said.

'It's not fiction characters who are heartless,' his father said, pretending to direct a glare at Beth. 'It's certain fiction critics who take my work apart on my word processor.'

Beth made a face at him.

'Seriously, Dad. Why do heroes always have to behave like programmed machines?'

'Because they're as dedicated as insects. They have
to be. They can't wander around aimlessly in a story.
They have to be consumed by their goals. They have
to worry about them constantly. That's what fiction is
basically about. About goals and worry. It's certainly
about worry for me.'

Nick persisted. 'But why must heroes be so limited?'

'If you'd been listening to me in class, Nick, you
would have heard me talk about this very subject,' Beth
said in a schoolteacher tone of voice, unable to stop
herself. 'Stories can be as fantastic as their authors care
to make them, but they are governed by their own
internal logic and consistency, by laws as rigid as those
of nature. Story heroes are governed by their natures
and cannot act against them as we do.'

'That's a pity,' Nick said. 'It makes them so predictable.'

'I can see we're going to have wonderful literary
evenings, with two writers and an English literature
teacher,' Nick's father said cheerfully.

It was a novel feeling going to his father's wedding. It
wasn't a church wedding. It happened in a Registry
Office, a sort of courtroom lined with wood panels and
with rows of bench seats, and official seals stuck on the
walls — a place where Nick would have expected
people to be put on trial, rather than to be joined in
marriage.

The bride wore a black-and-white cocktail dress and a white veil that attached to a small black-and-white hat on her hair. When Nick saw her coming down the aisle he felt a void open up inside him. The white veil over her face threw a mysterious haze over her features. It reminded him of something. It was a hollow feeling of loneliness inside him, a gap where something had once been. He wondered what made him feel that way.

The magistrate suited his address to a courtroom. He spoke the way Nick expected a divorce lawyer to speak. He said nothing about love. He said marriage was a contract involving his and her rights and that it was all about splitting responsibilities and about separate growth.

'You'll notice he doesn't mention God, sacrifice or serving each other,' Nick's grandfather, Popper, commented in a growling aside to him. Popper had certain firmly held beliefs about life and its meaning. Popper was a big, bear-like man with broad, kind eyes. He looked like a deep-sea fisherman whose face was weathered by the wind and the ocean, even though he did not like boats and fished instead from the rocks.

It was only later after the wedding and the reception, held at a local hotel reception room, when Nick waved his father and Beth goodbye as they left on their honeymoon trip on Kangaroo Island, that Nick remembered. The sight of Beth in the veil had reminded him of a photograph of his mother and father on their wedding day. It was a picture that stood on a shelf in his father's study. His grandfather, who had moved into their bluestone home, drove Nick back in a blue pick-up. 'You seem down, Nick,' he said. 'They'll soon be back.'

'I'll get along on my own.'

'Not exactly on your own. We're never on our own.'

'Sorry. You'll be there.'

'I don't mean me, either.'

'Then who do you mean?'

'Somebody you know about.'

'Ah.'

'Never think you're entirely on your own, Nick. Even when there are no people around.'

Nick went into his father's study to look at the photograph on the mantelpiece. It had gone. He stared at the blank spot where it usually stood. His father had not even bothered to wipe the mantelpiece clean. The dust still held the memory of where the photograph had stood all those years. Had his father, diplomatically, put it away, not wishing to upset his new bride? Or had he thrown it out? Nick knew that he should have understood, but he felt as if his father had discarded their past and he felt himself trembling with anger.

'You're not burying my mother,' he said. He scratched among shelves and in drawers until he found the familiar photograph of his father and his mother on their wedding day. It lay in a drawer in a thin gold frame with tarnished corners.

It wasn't the usual posed group-shot of a couple and their relatives standing outside a church, screwing their eyes shut against bright sunlight. One of his father's friends had been a fashion photographer and he had taken a moody shot of the two of them at the ceremony before his mother had lifted her white veil. It was the only photograph left of his mother. The rest had been lost in a packing crate when they had moved house.

His mother was dressed in flowing, hazy white. He

couldn't quite see his mother's face through the veil, but the gentle curves of nose and eyes and smiling mouth told him that she was very beautiful. It had seemed to him as a small boy that looking at her photograph was like looking at an angel through clouds. If only he could move that veil aside, he could know her completely. But he never could do that. He would always be left to wonder.

Nick put the photograph back on the mantelpiece gently, although with a sense of defiance.

'Back to your rightful place,' he said.

How could his father have done it? If only his father had married someone other than Beth Ryder, it would have been easy to hate them both.

The next day, Kate was full of questions about the wedding or, more particularly, about Beth.

'What did Miss Ryder look like?'

'She isn't Miss Rider any more; she's Mrs Lawrence Young,' he said.

'Never mind that. Did she wear white? What was her dress like?'

'I don't know. Black-and-white, I think.'

'And her shoes?'

'I didn't see any shoes.'

'No shoes at her wedding?' Kate said sarcastically.

'I mean I didn't notice any shoes, that's all.'

'Think. Were they white or black?' Nick couldn't remember. 'Boys! I don't suppose you noticed her bouquet; that's too much to ask.' Bouquet? Did Kate think he was a fashion reporter? 'Didn't you notice *anything* important?' she said. 'You're not very observant for a writer, are you?'

'Well, they weren't important things,' he said. 'Only

dumb details.'

'Only to a boy they're dumb details,' she said in a superior voice. 'I'll make it easy for you,' she said, finally. 'I'll boil it down into one simple, all-important question: did she look beautiful?'

'I can't honestly say.'

Kate locked him in her narrow gaze. 'The truth, Nick.'

'She looked pretty okay to me,' he said, shrugging evasively.

'Pretty okay? And you call yourself a writer! Think about the way she looked and try to remember.'

A picture of her coming down the aisle of the Registry Office came back into his mind. Beth had looked pretty enough to make an angel cry, he thought, remembering the veil with the black-and-white hat and her shining black hair. Kate saw the answer in his face.

'She was beautiful, all right,' Kate said in a flat, resigned tone. 'She would be. Brides always are.'

6

The boat trip

NICK MISSED THE WORD PROCESSOR, perhaps as much as he missed his father. It was his anchor.

But he did not stop writing. He made himself write in an old exercise book on the empty desk in his father's study where the word processor had sat. He would transfer it to a disk on the word processor later when he arrived on the island. Their island. And now his father and Beth were enjoying it instead of him.

He also missed Beth secretly, even though he had left the old wedding picture of his mother and father on the shelf in his father's study in protest.

With Beth away, the class had a substitute teacher for English, the headmaster Mr Parry, who immediately set new books for the class to read, books which Nick refused to read. Mr Parry threatened to test them on these books 'at any tick of the clock'.

Nick's grandfather noticed his scribbling industry one morning. Nick sat at his father's empty computer desk in the study, writing in a ruled exercise book.

'What are you writing, Nick? You seem very keen on homework,' Popper said, bulking over him.

'A story, Popper. I write stories.'

'Do you now? Following in your dad's footsteps. What do you write about?'

'Heroes.'

'Ah. And who are they? Who are your heroes?'

'I like Flite Madison, a flying hero.'

Popper had a faintly bullying air, but a kind nature. His face, creased by days spent fishing off the rocks of the Encounter Coast, softened in a smile of surprise.

'You're old-fashioned, Nick. Personally, I prefer movie heroes like Indiana Jones, but if you're going to worship heroes there's one who leaves them all for dead.'

'Who's that?'

'He was the Light of the World and he lived by his wits, surrounded by enemies. In the end he sacrificed himself for others. He's the only hero who promised never to leave us. He'll be with us always until the end of time and you can always call on him. I've got his book. You should read it some time.'

Nick remembered the book. He had looked at it once. Popper kept it by his bedside. It was a battered black book with tissue-thin, gold-edged pages that were fine as insects' wings and almost as transparent. 'Some other time, Popper.'

'You're not upset about this marriage business? I couldn't help noticing that you've put your father's old wedding photograph on display again.'

'I can't help wondering what my mum would think.'

'I don't think she'd like it if she were here, but she's not here, so I guess where she is, she's perfectly happy about it. If heaven's half the place we think it is, there'll be more than enough consolations. There are some interesting people who've gone there ahead of her. Milton, Mozart, Michelangelo, Bach and the hero I mentioned before, except he's not only there; he's here, too.'

'I've got to finish this piece, Popper.'

'You go ahead. I'm going fishing. Always fishing, that's me. See you after school.'

The headmaster Mr Parry handed back their book tests. He stopped at Nick's desk, holding his essay in his hand.

'It requires a boy with great ingenuity to summarise a classic novel in two words, but that's what you've achieved with *Bleak House* by Charles Dickens. Your essay, Young, is a masterpiece of condensation.'

'Thankyou, Mr Parry.'

'Unlike the rest of the class, you were not side-tracked by character analysis, exploration of plot construction or of the novel's themes. You wrote a one page essay about the weather conditions around *Bleak House*. It reads as tersely as a meteorological report.'

'I felt it was a central metaphor, Sir,' Nick said, thinking quickly. 'And Charles Dickens obviously agreed. He chose it as his title.'

'But I think he meant you to read more than the title, Young. And that's obviously all you've done. All you have taken out of this classic is two words, "Bleak" and "House". Did you sample the book at all?'

Actually he had, Nick recalled. He had opened it up at the middle in his usual way and given the book a sniff or two. He hadn't liked what he'd discovered. It was crammed cheek-by-jowl with jostling characters and it smelt as stifling as a crowded bus in the rush hour. An *omni*bus, to put it in Dickens' time.

'You can stay behind for an extra two hours every afternoon until you have actually read *Bleak House* and are equipped to write a decent essay.'

'But the book's hundreds of pages long.'

'Precisely,' Mr Parry said, smiling maliciously.

'Poor Nick,' Kate murmured beside him.

Nothing was going well for him.

After school, Nick sat in the classroom reading *Bleak House*. The words and the characters danced teasingly in front of his eyes, demanding his attention, but one half of him resisted. He kept remembering his vow never to read ever again and it made progress slow.

He broke away and looked longingly out of the window at the sky. He wanted to be out there flying his Supermarine.

But there would be no more flying until he had finished this book. He went reluctantly back to reading *Bleak House*.

His punishment went on for a week, every afternoon. Perhaps Mr Parry hated him, he thought, because his father had married the school's best English teacher and taken her away. Now Mr Parry was taking it out on Nick.

Nick read almost to the end of *Bleak House* that night, before he fell asleep in his bed and the book fell on his nose. He dreamt he was riding in a Victorian omnibus. It was stifling, crammed with characters in squeezed bonnets and top hats who were being as eccentric as they could be.

Only a few pages remained to be read the next day. Kate waved him goodbye after class and he settled down to finish the book. Fifty-four minutes later, exactly, he was finished and he slammed *Bleak House* triumphantly shut. Even *Bleak House* had to come to an end.

He reported to the headmaster's office, carrying *Bleak House* with him under an arm. Mr Parry was doing some paperwork in his office when he knocked at the frosted glass door. Mr Parry did not look up.

'Come in, Young.' Lit from behind by the light of a window, Mr Parry looked more like a mad scientist than a headmaster with unruly clown's hair like bright clouds on either side of his head. He viewed Nick with disfavour now as he came in and stood in front of his desk.

'You've read more than the title this time.'

'I've read it all, Sir.'

'It helps.' Mr Parry glanced at a clock on the wall of his office. 'But you can't go home yet. You have another hour's detention to go. Go back to your classroom and write me an appreciation of *Bleak House*. We'll see what you know.'

Nick slumped. 'Yes, Mr Parry.'

'Leave the book here.'

He put the book on Mr Parry's desk.

He went back to the classroom, took out some sheets of paper and began to write. He hardly mentioned the weather conditions around *Bleak House*. He wrote a good piece with perceptive observations about the story and its characters and he was proud of it.

Mr Parry came to collect it at the end of the hour. Nick handed the five pages to him with a confident flourish. Perhaps this would please the headmaster. Nick fully expected it to delight Mr Parry.

Mr Parry took the five page essay from him. Hot

from the walk to the classroom, he idly fanned himself with it. 'Why didn't you do this in the first place, Young?' Then, without reading it, Mr Parry tore the essay in two and dropped it into a wastepaper basket on his way out.

Things were not going well, Nick thought.

He felt even less like reading books.

He went back to the Hobby Hangar to see Des.

There was a sign in the window. It said: 'Under New Management'.

He asked the new owner about Des. The man shrugged. Des had sold the business and gone. Nobody knew where.

Did Nick want to buy something? The shop had a special introductory offer on glider kits. 'No thanks,' said Nick.

The phone rang one afternoon. It was the man who had repaired the boy's plane.

The man spoke in a harsh whisper. 'You've still got the plane I fixed?'

'Is that you, Des?'

'Yes. There's something you must know about that plane. It's a military. . . argh. . . secret of great importance to the argh. . . argh!'

'Do you have a sore throat, Des? It sounds as if you're gargling.' *Des probably had one of those fancy cordless phones that he could take with him to his bathroom. It didn't surprise him about Des. A man who once owned the Hobby Hangar shop had to have a soft spot for gadgets.*

'What are you saying, Des?'

'Argh!'

'Des? Why don't you phone me back when you've finished gargling?'

'Argh.'

Was that agreement? 'Des?'

'Just take great care of it. Everyone will be after. . . it. . . especially the argh. . .'

'The Argh?'

'No, the. . . argh.'

'The Argentinians?'

'Aaaargh!'

After a particularly emphatic gargle, the phone and possibly Des himself, judging by the sound of the thump that followed, went dead. Perhaps Des ought to change his brand of throat gargle. It was a bit strong.

They drove to Jervis Bay where they caught a catamaran vehicle and passenger ferry to Penneshaw on Kangaroo Island.

Someone had boarded the ferry to make contact with the boy.

While the old man and the girl sat on the upper deck on the way over, the boy went to a small refreshment canteen below decks where he ordered a cold drink. He sat at one of the tables at a window facing forward, looking out at the hazy, green-blanket spread of Kangaroo Island that crept closer to them, growing in detail as if he were viewing it through a slowly focussing lens.

It was a funny thing, he reflected, but Kangaroo Island actually looked bigger than the Australian mainland when you were halfway across the passage. Kangaroo Island was a sizeable land mass, over a hundred kilometres long and fifty wide, a place of wild rampart cliffs, lighthouses and powder-soft beaches. It was also an island ark stocked with rare animals trapped thousands of years ago when a landbridge which once joined it to the mainland sank beneath the waters of the Backstairs Passage. It was the way Australia used to be 10,000 years ago.

A stranger brought a cup of coffee to the boy's table and without invitation slipped into a chair across from him.

'Going through with the flight?' the man said.

The boy gave him a frown. The stranger had a lean, brown, wily face with a lateral scar across one cheek.

'What flight? Who are you?'

'Somebody who is watching you. You're getting into very dangerous water. You mustn't do what they ask.'

The dark young man blew on his coffee to cool it, then sipped it.

'Let me guess. You're Security,' the boy said. 'ASIO?'

The man swallowed, almost choked. He screwed up his face. 'Sorry,' the boy apologised, quickly looking around. 'Did I say that too loudly?'

'It's not what you said. It's this canteen coffee. I'm a bit of a connoisseur about my food and drink.'

'Who exactly are they?' the boy asked him.

The man shook his head. 'Sorry, "they" is something we'd rather not talk about. But I can tell you something about the one who contacted you. He's part of a team working on a secret project at South Australia's Technology Park, home of the defence establishment. They have been testing model prototypes of some sort. A secret defence development. Something has been stolen by a member of the development team. The one who contacted you.'

'The doctor.'

He gave an ironically bitter smile. *'The doctor, yes, but he's no medical doctor and if he suspects you're crossing him he could be bad for your health. He'll do anything to get this secret out of the country, even recruit a kid. We know him by another name, of course. What did he ask you to do?'*

'Why would they ask me to do anything?'

'We can guess. They want you to do some offshore flying. They want you to fly a plane off a cliff at night to a waiting submarine.'

'Wow. That would be exciting.'

'Exciting for the Western World if our enemy got hold of the secret.'

'Who exactly is the enemy these days?' the boy asked, innocently. *'I thought the Russians were turning friendly.'*

'I'd rather not talk about that, either. It's top secret.'

'You mean our enemies are top secret?'

'Tops.'

'I thought only spies were top secret?'

'Countries, too,' he said.

'Imagine a top secret country!' The boy supposed it was safer that way. You had to keep your enemies a secret these days because countries had a habit of changing sides so quickly you risked offending them if you came out and called them enemies.

'Just don't go through with it.'

'I don't know what you're talking about. Who'd believe that a boy would be asked to fly out a military secret?'

'I believe it. And so do the guys out there. Take a look.' He pointed out to sea.

The boy narrowed his eyes and peered. Out on the silver glare of the horizon he saw a floating steel mountain that could only be a Nimitz class US aircraft carrier. A jet was streaking off the deck.

The boy shrugged. 'So Australia and America are having military exercises. So what?'

'Everyone's watching this island. And you.'

'Where have you been, Nick?' Kate said, sitting on a white bench on the deck of the catamaran ferry, her red hair streaming in a twenty-knot wind and a paperback book she had brought to read flapping like a trapped bird in her hand. Popper sat beside her, looking a little green with the lurching of the vessel.

'I've been below decks for a walk around.' He turned to his grandfather. 'Would you like a drink, Popper? Something to eat? They've got a canteen below with cut sandwiches and cream buns.'

Popper groaned. Nick looked at Kate.

'No thanks,' Kate said. There was a trace of irritation in her voice. 'You're not going to keep on disappearing, are you? I'm not sitting around on Kangaroo Island on my own.'

'Of course not.'

'Why don't you sit down?'

He thought about it, not sure what he wanted to do. 'Come on, Nick, don't be so restless.'

He joined Popper and Kate on the white bench seat. Kate smiled at Nick. 'You're not going to spend all your time swaggering around like a tough guy, are you? You look like a biker in that jacket.'

'It's not a biker's jacket. It just shows what girls know. It's a flying jacket.'

'I'm only teasing. Are you nervous?' she said. 'About finding your teacher there with your father?'

'I'll get used to the idea.'

'Is that why you wanted me to come with you? You wanted a girl along to balance things out. You wouldn't be trying to make the teacher jealous?' she said, watching Nick carefully. 'Because that would be very silly. She's a grown woman, Nick, and you're a boy and she's only interested in you in a motherly way. I hope you see that. Don't hug any dumb ideas to yourself. I know how impressionable teenage boys can get.'

Stung, Nick hit back. 'I noticed a few teenage girls being impressionable about Mr Shaw, the science master.'

'Mr Shaw is rather nice,' she said, her eyes flashing guiltily, 'but I for one didn't have any silly ideas.'

'Well, neither do I,' he said hotly. The awful thing about Kate was that she looked right into you as if you were just a pane of glass. 'There's only one thought in my mind about Beth. I want to show her. I'm going to continue writing until I convince her that I can write. Then I'll be satisfied.'

Kate gave Nick a sad, superior smile and went back to reading her book. Popper's face was looking greener than Kangaroo Island.

7

The lighthouse keeper

FROM THE WHARF AT THE SMALL seaside village of Penneshaw, they drove in Popper's blue pick-up to a rented Cornish-style stone cottage that looked out over a cobalt stretch of the Backstairs Passage. It also overlooked two smaller islands called The Pages.

Their holiday cottage lay in a direct line right between them. Nick remarked on it to his grandfather in a low voice so that Kate couldn't hear: 'I've just realised something, Popper. Do you know that for the next two weeks we'll be living between The Pages?'

'Not a bad place for a writer to be,' his grandfather said smiling as he stopped his pick-up outside the cottage. 'As long as he's living in the right book.'

Nick's father and Beth came out of the cottage to greet them.

The two looked tanned and happy, his father dressed in shorts and a T-shirt and Beth in a white flowing skirt and a tie-top white blouse. Beth greeted Kate warmly and kissed Nick on the cheek. 'I'm glad you've brought Kate with you, Nick,' she whispered in his ear. She had the summery, sweet coconut smell of suntan lotion on her skin. 'Still wearing your leather jacket like an airman?'

Was she really glad he had brought Kate, or just saying it? It unsettled him. Why was she glad? Perhaps she thought the bookish Kate would be a good influence on him.

'I'll show you your room, Kate,' Beth said. 'Then I'll take you around.' With the air of a hostess, she took Kate on a guided tour of the cottage. She acted as if it were her place, Nick thought with a twinge of resentment.

'I'll berth myself in the back verandah, as usual,' Popper said. He liked to stay in the small enclosed verandah at the back. It had its own door so that he could slip out at all hours to go fishing without waking up the rest of the house.

The holiday cottage was going to be as jam-packed with characters as a Dickens novel, Nick thought, taking his case and his aeroplane to his bedroom. He put the float plane on top of a wooden dressing table and looked around the place, a plain room with rendered stone walls painted in cream. The room had a faintly musty smell and pine floorboards. A single window looked over the water and The Pages.

The Pages.

He felt pressed between them like an insect squashed in a book.

The room looked the same, yet it felt different knowing Beth was in the house and knowing that she must have visited his room. He remembered what Kate had said about the shower and about his new stepmother's cosmetics and bottles collecting there. Had Beth taken over there, too? Nick felt an urge to find out, even before he unpacked. He went to the shower to check.

Kate had been right. A collection of pink and green bottles, shampoos, conditioners and rinses stood on the tiled floor of the shower. Nick stared at the array in horror.

'What's the matter, Nick? Found a spider in our shower?' Beth said, laughing, as she came behind him to the bathroom door, with Kate in tow.

'Just seeing if things are still the same,' he said, looking trapped.

Kate knew exactly what was going through his mind. She tried to catch Nick's eye. He avoided her as he went out. He knew that she'd be smiling in a superior Kate way.

Next he went to see where his father had put the word processor. He discovered it sitting on a small table tucked in an alcove off the kitchen. That was good. It was easy to reach. At least it wasn't in his father's bedroom. That could have made things tricky.

Nick went back to his bedroom to unpack his things into a small wooden chest of drawers.

There was a tap at the door. Beth.

'Hi,' he said weakly. He swallowed.

She came in, smiling, and closed the door after her. 'I wanted to have a private word with you, Nick. May I sit on the bed?'

Oh no, he thought. Beth this close, in a confined space! She didn't even have her reading glasses on! Where would he look? She sat on the corner of his bed. 'Sit down a moment. You can unpack later.'

'I'd rather stand,' he said, his heart beating wildly. 'I've been sitting all the way over on the ferry.'

She nodded. 'I understand. I just wanted to say how lovely it is to have you with us. Your father has missed you and I've been looking forward to you — and Kate — joining us. I think we can have a wonderful time — in fact a wonderful life — together. I want you to forget that I was your teacher. I won't be for much longer, by the way, since I think it's best if I moved to another school. Please think of me as a friend. I'm really not so fearsome, you know.'

'I never thought that,' he said, continuing to unpack his suitcase and nervously dropping a rolled- up pair of socks. He scooped them up.

'That's a lovely aeroplane,' she said admiringly. The float plane sat on top of the dressing table, like a fighter on an aircraft carrier, looking braced and eager to spring into the air. 'I'm glad you're going to relax a bit and enjoy yourself. I hope you've brought some books to read. I notice Kate has brought a small library in her suitcase.'

'I won't be reading,' he said firmly. It came out a little more forcefully than he had meant.

She blinked in surprise. 'I don't mean schoolwork, Nick. I'm not a schoolteacher twenty-four hours a day, you know. I mean books for pleasure.'

'There'll be other things I'll do for pleasure,' he told her.

'As you like. But just unwind and enjoy life.'

'I hope you and my dad are happy,' he managed to say, out of politeness.

'Thankyou, Nick. We are. Very.'

'That's good then.'

He was relieved when she left. And forlorn.

Kate came to the door.

'So this is your room. You can't hide from me in here. Show me the beach.'

For their first lunch together, Beth, with his father and Kate's help, prepared salads and sliced cold meats served with fresh baked island bread.

'How's the writing going?' Popper asked conversationally as they ate.

'Fine,' Nick said. Too late he saw that Popper was looking at his father.

'He writes me under the table,' Nick's father complained, turning his eyes to Nick. 'My work's obviously not going as well as Nick's. Mind you, Beth tries to keep me at it. She's not a schoolteacher for nothing.'

'Don't say that, Lawrence,' Beth said chidingly. 'I've just told Nick to forget that I'm a schoolteacher. And that goes for you, too, Kate. I'm Beth while you're here. Forget school.'

'What school?' Kate said. 'I've forgotten about it already.'

'I wish Beth would let me out of school,' his father said.

'Only when you've finished the first draft of your book.'

Nick could not help staring at Beth at their table. It took some getting used to.

Kate noticed and watched Nick's eyes. It made him feel uncomfortable because it meant he couldn't stare at Beth and steep himself in the strangeness of it all. Kate nudged him with a foot under the table and gave a teasing smile.

'What are we all doing after lunch?' his father said.

'You're writing,' Beth said firmly.

'I'm fishing,' Popper said.

'I'm still a bit wobbly after the ferry trip,' Kate said. 'I think I'd like to stretch out somewhere and read. On the beach. What about you, Nick?'

'I *don't* want to read.'

Beth noticed the sharpness in his voice and tried to find an answer first in Nick's face then in Kate's. Kate shrugged. Beth tried his father next, but found no answer there.

'Authors never read enough,' his father said.

It was the second time Beth had heard Nick dismiss the idea of reading in an angry tone. Beth grew thoughtful.

'Why don't you sit on the beach with me, Nick,' Kate said, 'and keep me company?'

'While you read? I'd rather fly my plane.'

'I hope it isn't noisy.'

'It sounds like a thousand amplified dentist's drills going off at once inside your head,' his father said encouragingly.

'It's not that bad,' Nick said.

'Do I really have to write?' his father said, turning to Beth.

'You do, Lawrence. The sooner you've finished, the sooner we can spend more time together. And don't forget you have to go to the mainland for that meeting in a few days' time.'

If only Beth encouraged his writing like that, Nick thought enviously. If only somebody did.

Nick stood on a grassy knoll above a stretch of sunlit beach and brought his float plane around in a gentle bank and took it low over the figure of the girl who lay reading a book and sunning herself on a red-and-white towel beside an open umbrella. She twisted her head to look up at the passing blue-and-white streak.

He went through aerobatic patterns, tight Outside Loops, easy Four Point Rolls, a stylish Cuban Eight. Next he cut circles in the sky as he went through an immaculate Horizontal Eight. He let it spiral downwards in a breathtaking Falling Leaf, made a dead level recovery and now pointed its nose up. Would he dare risk a Tail Slide with Kate watching?

The little float plane arrowed up, the afternoon sun striking spangles off its gleaming wings. Higher and higher it went, piercing the belly of the sky. It spluttered. Its power almost died. For a while its momentum carried it skyward, then it paused, lost inertia and began to slide down its climbing track. Nick sent a pulse out to the small aircraft that was dropping like a stone.

It quivered. Its powerplant lifted in pitch as its tiny airscrews whined. It was in a spin and he struggled to right it, calling on all of the controls. He brought it out of it, put it in a bank and ran it low over the girl's head.

He expected some polite applause at least.

Kate scowled, dropped her book and covered her ears with her hands as the little float plane ground the air above her head. She made signals for him to fly it somewhere else.

Nick shrugged, then went further down the beach. No appreciation. Girls obviously did not understand the skills involved in aerobatic flying. He moved the tiny levers and set the float plane's nose on a course along the beach. He wondered if he could land it safely at some distance down the beach, aiming for a spot where the waves ran flatly up the powder-white sand.

He fed in some down trim and cut back to half throttle and brought it down. The Supermarine bellied with some frame-jarring smacks, but it was sturdily constructed and it survived. He turned it around to taxi it in to the shore. It came in, tail wagging, up the beach.

It was a long walk to retrieve it. He had better hurry before the waves carried it out, he thought. Nick collapsed the whip aerial on the transmitter and took off the harness, leaving it on the grassy knoll so that he would be free to run.

He need not have bothered.

Somebody beat him to it.

A man walked to the water's edge and picked up his tiny aircraft. He threw a look in Nick's direction.

Nick stopped after no more than a few steps. The man walked towards Nick along the stretch of beach, carrying his aircraft through the shivery heat. The wingtips flared like mirror signals, making Nick blink.

He looked at Kate lying on the beach. She had not seen him. Her nose was still buried in a book. It was quieter now without the whining sound of the float plane's engine filling the air. He heard the dump and hiss of the waves on the beach. The sound washed over him, lulling him. He felt removed from the scene. The man came closer. He was a sinewy-looking man with hair like windblown straw. He carried the Supermarine in his arms like a cross in a procession and he came forward with a shy smile on his sunburnt face.

'Always wanted to meet a boy who could fly,' he

said. 'That was pretty fancy flying. What's your name, son?'

'I'm Nick. Thanks for bringing my plane.'

He gave Nick his aeroplane. 'I couldn't let you lose your wings. I was taking a walk when I saw you put down. I'm the keeper.'

'You operate the *lighthouse*? Cape Willoughby lighthouse? It must be lonely keeping a lighthouse,' Nick said.

He shrugged. 'Not really. You think of those out there depending on your light. It's a link.'

'I've always wondered about lighthouse keepers. What makes you do a job like that?'

'Nothing. You choose it.'

'Is that what you're best at doing?'

'There are some other things I do better, but I choose to do this.' He spoke in a very easy, unemphatic way. 'What about you? I see you're pretty good at flying model planes. But what will you choose to do?'

His clear blue eyes searched Nick's face as they must have searched the horizon for ships at night. It was a small hook of a question, yet it bit curiously deep in Nick's mind. He felt that he could neither ignore it nor wriggle free from it. It demanded an answer and he felt that he could trust this man with the answer.

'I want to fly and also to write stories.'

The man thought about that. 'I'm sure that you do both very well, but what do you want to achieve with these skills? Can they be made to do some good? There's a difference between having skills and choosing good causes.'

'I can decide that later. First, I need experience. Before I can write, I have to experience life — everything. I have to gather all the experiences I can.' Nick wanted to know the answer to something and he sensed that this stranger was one person who could give it to him.

The man shrugged.

'Be a bit careful about that. You can't do just anything in life in the name of gathering experiences.'

'I'm not gathering them for myself, but so that I can write better and convince people.'

'Who do you want to convince?'

'People who don't think I can do it.'

'I wouldn't doubt you,' he said. He spoke as if he knew Nick and, curiously, it felt as if he did. 'Maybe I'll see you again, son.' The stranger went back up the beach. 'Happy landings.'

Nick trudged disconsolately over the sand to Kate who put down her book.

'Where have you been? I told you I wasn't sitting around on my own on this island.'

'Sorry. I almost lost my aeroplane and had to go after it.'

She lay under the umbrella and he went gratefully into its shade to join her, putting down the float plane and the transmitter.

'What's wrong, Nick? You look worried.'

'Nothing.' He glanced at her book. 'Been reading, I see.'

'Very observant. I haven't given up reading. I wish you hadn't. Why don't you relax and read a book? It's too warm to be out flying. And why are you wearing that silly jacket? You must be roasting.'

'Do you believe in story characters, Kate?'

'That's a funny thing to ask. I believe in them if the

writer's written about them well enough.'

'I mean, do you think they're a good example to follow?'

She thought about it. 'Well, in some ways. They're pretty determined about overcoming obstacles to reach their goals and I suppose that's something to admire in them.'

'Yes, but that's all they care about. They don't think about anything else.'

'They can't. Their writers won't let them. They have to behave the way their creators say so.'

'So they don't care about anyone else. They don't care about you and me.'

'What a weird thing to say. All this writing you're doing is starting to get to you.'

'Perhaps,' Nick said. 'I suppose I've always expected too much of heroes.'

'Maybe you've had the wrong ones,' Kate said.

Now she was sounding like Popper.

'Seen Popper?'

'He's down at the rocks fishing.'

'Think I'll go and say hello.'

Nick took his aeroplane and transmitter with him and he trudged along the sand to find Popper.

8

Popper

'HOW'S THE BOY AUTHOR?' Popper said. He swung his fishing rod expertly, hurling out the heavy lead weight at the end of the line like a stone from a catapult. It made a small spout of water where it hit the ocean.

'You're very good at that.'

'It's a sign of a misspent youth, middle age and old age, I'm afraid. What's on your mind, Nick?'

'Oh nothing.'

'Just. . .?'

'A question.'

'What question?' The old man wound in a few feet of line until it was drawn taut and slipped the reel onto the ratchet.

'About that hero you mentioned. He cares about those who count on him?'

'Enough to die for them.'

'Not like some heroes I know,' he said.

Popper was a burly, bearded old man who stood with his broad sandalled feet widely placed on the rock to help him keep his balance. A heavy metal box of fishing tackle sat on the rock at his feet. He considered Nick through gently hooded eyes, creased at the corners. 'You look to me like a boy who has lost something,' he said.

'I haven't lost anything, but I'm looking for something.'

'I know,' he said. 'You're looking for a hero.'

'How do you know?'

'All boys are looking for heroes. But a real hero is hard to find. In fact, you never really find your real hero. He finds you. It's a bit like fishing.' He gave the long fishing rod in his brown hands a flick and a ripple ran down its length. 'You bait the hook and you cast the line, but do you choose the fish or does it choose you?'

'I choose my heroes,' Nick said.

'Perhaps. Will you hold the rod for me for a while? I'll take a rest.'

'What if a big fish comes along?'

'Then we'll see how you go.'

He handed the rod to Nick. It was as tall as a church spire. 'Take in a bit of slack here,' he told him and he showed him how to work the reel and keep a testing finger on the line before he sat nearby on a rock and stretched out his legs.

The line trembled in Nick's fingers. The line out at sea was alive with thrummings and stirrings. He felt as if he were holding a lightning rod in an underwater storm. Waves rumbled and burst their bellies in showers near his feet.

'Feel yourself out there in the deep,' Popper said in a voice that rumbled like the waves. 'Imagine yourself seeing below the surface. Blink and peer through the spume. There are creatures of shadow down there and also one giant silvery fish that shines in light. What do you want to catch?'

'The giant one, of course.'

'What will you use to tempt him?'

'Juicy bait.'

'What exactly is bait? Define it.'

'Prawn.'

'No, define the word "bait". What is it?'

'Bait is something you offer to lure a fish.'

'And what does "offering" mean?'

'Giving something.'

'Yes, giving something.' Popper's eyes looked inwards into himself. The boy had the feeling that the old man could picture the bottom of the sea in his mind. 'I see two fish swimming towards your bait,' he said. 'One is dark and shadowy and full of sinister power. But he is very exciting, deadly and angular, a racer of the deep. The other is a giant source of silvery light that floods the ocean where he swims. Little fish follow him, dancing ecstatically in his light like moths around a lamp. He knows everything, this big fish, even why you are here and what it is that you want. What will you give up to win him?'

'All my bait.'

'He wants more than a piece of prawn. He is going to demand that you give your all to get him, that you do things a certain way and don't do other things. He sniffs the bait, nibbles it gently, then what does he do? He gives himself utterly. He hooks *himself* by swallowing your bait.'

Something heavy bumped the line. Then the line twanged tautly like a guitar string.

'I've got him.'

'Are you sure? Maybe he's got you. Pull gently to hook him more tightly. Now don't try to yank him bodily in to you. You must get used to his power. He will give himself to you, if you respect his power and go easily.'

The boy felt the rod and line crackle as if lightning had struck it and a force ran up his arms that made the hairs stand out on them. He pulled gently. The rod quivered and jerked. He had hooked a lightning bolt.

The fish struck. No, he decided, it wasn't a lightning bolt. He had hooked an underwater storm. The unseen fish ran with swirling power.

'Let him go. You can't hope to hold him.' The line screamed out of the reel like Nick's float plane in a dive. On and on the big fish ran with the line. 'How much will he take?'

'Everything. Until he senses that you will give him all you have. Then he will start giving to you in return. He will give himself, the ultimate prize.'

Take all you want, Nick radioed to him.

The pull slackened. The fish stopped.

'Try pulling gently,' the old man said.

He pulled, trying to wind the handle of the reel. He might as well have been trying to wind in the mainland. But then the catch came, very easily towards him. He was gripped suddenly by a fear.

'I can't.'

'Are you afraid that you can't hold on?'

'He's a bit much for me. I don't have your strength. I'm only a kid.'

'Hang on. You can do it.'

'I don't want to. You take it.'

Strong hands took the rod from Nick's hands.

'It sometimes happens like that,' he said. 'But he'll always be there now that you've held onto him, even if it was only for a moment or two.'

The fish had gone. He must have shaken himself off the line. Popper reeled in his line and found that his bait had been eaten.

The waves fell on the rocks like endless curling questions. Nick's search for guidance had also fallen on stony ground, he thought.

He stayed to rest a while, watching Popper fishing off the rocks. He chose a smooth, raised shelf of rock behind him to sit on, resting his aircraft and transmitter on the rock beside him.

He thought about the stranger who had given him the jacket and about the other flier, the one he read about in books. Shouldn't you look up to heroes and do what they did? If you couldn't look up to your heroes, who could you look up to? If you couldn't follow their example, whose example could you follow?

What was a hero? Nick had looked it up in the dictionary once: '1. A man who is admired for his brave and noble deeds. 2. The chief male character in a story.' The heroes he admired were risk takers, but they weren't all that noble. Did anybody want goody-goody heroes any more? Readers wanted a bit of shadow as well as light because pure light was a bit tiring to look at for long, and shadow gave things form and mystery. Was it the same in life? Nick wasn't so sure. Shadows were one thing in a story, but who wanted shadows in their life?

The boy felt pulled in different directions by two urges. His dilemma was clear to him. If he failed to go through with the flight he would not have the story to tell and so would fail

*to convince others of his writing skills. But if he did go
through with the flight, he would probably be making a choice
that was bad.*

*Perhaps some of the most heroic things in real life weren't
actions, but resisting actions, he thought. It didn't make for
adventure, but it probably made for a good clean feeling inside
you, which was not the way he felt right then.*

He felt as buffeted as the rocks and churned up as
the waves around Popper. Nick picked up some flat
pebbles and skipped them over the waves that boiled
around the rocks. The movement caught Popper's eye.
Nick thought he would complain about him scaring
away the fish, but instead he smiled.

It was while Popper was turned that a giant wave
curved over the rock and swept over him and sucked
him back out with it. Nick saw him go down in the
water and come up again. He saw the wild surprise in
the old man's drenched face, the sea streaming down
his wet beard and hair on his forehead in the water.
Then he disappeared again in the next wave. He came
up again, then another surge of spumy sea rolled over
him.

'Help!' Nick yelled as loudly as he could, twisting
around. A breeze smothered his shout like a hand.
Nick stood on the rock to look for help. Was the
lighthouse keeper still in view? The empty beach
looked blankly back at him. Kate was there, but she
hadn't seen what had happened and was out of earshot.

Popper was going out further. He didn't seem to be
struggling any more, perhaps to save his strength or
because he was powerless to fight against such waves.

'What do I do?' Nick thought. He could swim, but
not well and probably not as strongly as Popper. He

could run to the cottage, but by the time he got back the old man would be lost from view. And what could anyone at the cottage do?

'I see you're pretty good at flying model planes,' the keeper had said. 'But what will you choose to do?'

'I want to fly and to write stories.'

The man had thought about that. 'I'm sure that you do both very well, but what do you want to achieve with these skills? Can they be made to do some good? There's a difference between having skills and choosing good causes.'

The seaplane.

He jumped down from the rock, taking his plane and the transmitter to the place where Popper had been standing. Popper's heavy metal box of fishing tackle was still sitting on the rock. His fingers shaky with excitement, Nick scratched inside the box for a length of rope and a lighter length of fishing line. He attached the fishing line to one of the Supermarine's floats and pulled out a length of it from a spool, attaching the other end to the rope which he secured to a protruding edge of rock.

He looked back to find Popper. Gone. Nick felt his hopes stall and go sliding back into despair. He was too late. Then he saw a pink face between the waves quite far out.

Nick started the float plane and went nearer to the edge where the briny breath of the ocean blew in his downturned face. It would have to be a hand launch — the water was too rough for a water take-off. He gave the engine throttle, holding it while it strained in his hand. He released it in a level glide and took it up. The Supermarine bucked in the updraught as an unseen

current of air hit it and Nick fought with the controls on
the box at his chest to steady it. Then it was climbing,
dragging a silver thread of line behind it. He hoped that
he had allowed enough line to reach Popper. The float
plane could tow lightweight fishing line, but not wet
rope. Popper must have seen what Nick was doing
because he gave a wave to signal his position more
clearly. Maybe this could be done. Maybe it could
really work. Nick flicked a glance down to the fishing
line uncoiling off the smooth rock beside him. At any
second it would end, the heavy rope would begin and
the float plane would stop as abruptly as if it had hit a
wall.

Nick fed in elevator to give the float plane height and
momentum. Then the fishing line twanged as it
engaged the heavy rope and the Supermarine came to
the end of its tether. It dropped into the sea, metres
short of Popper. A wave went over Popper's head. He
was going out further.

The float plane's engine was still going. Nick
grabbed a coil of the heavier rope and went right to the
edge of the rock where he hurled it out to help it on its
way.

Then he gave the Supermarine full throttle. Answering to the pulse from the transmitter, it tugged bravely,
waddling like a duck, inching out closer to Popper's
outstretched hand. It was getting there. He fed out
more rope. The wet rope would soon grow heavy,
perhaps heavy enough to drag the plane under, but it
kept going. Buoyed by the sight of help approaching,
Popper made an extra effort to strike out towards the
plane. The tide going out helped Nick. He gave the

engine more revs. He could hear its tiny screaming engine protesting as it strained towards the old man.

Then in a final spurt from both Popper and the float plane, they closed the gap and met. Popper found the fishing line and pulled, dragging the heavier rope towards him.

Nick let out more eagerly. It grew tight and trembled with the life at the end of it. The rest was remarkably easy. 'I wouldn't let you drown. You're safe now,' Nick said, helping to pull the old man back onto the rocks.

It was the catch of the day, Popper said afterwards.

It was the first time Nick had ever been treated as a hero. His father cooked a celebration barbecue that night. Beth and Kate made the salads. Popper and Nick put their feet up.

'He was magnificent,' Popper said. 'A real hero. Forget your books, Nick. That was real-life heroism.'

'Don't encourage him,' Kate said. 'He already swaggers around like an air ace in that leather jacket.'

'No, don't play it down. What happened was special. Nick showed great presence of mind, not to mention real flying skill. I owe young Nick and his little aeroplane my life — no doubt about it.'

'Well done, Nick,' Kate said. 'Just don't get a fat head over it.'

It was a good and rare feeling to feel the glow of approval, but the incident had made Nick think a lot. Being a hero wasn't quite the way he thought it would be. You didn't feel big, but very small and grateful that you had been lucky enough to play a part in something bigger than your own daily worries.

It made him think a lot about heroes, real ones and storybook ones.

'Speaking of books and heroes,' his father said after the meal, 'I'd better get back to work.'

'I'm glad to hear it,' Beth said. 'When I checked your work on the word processor last night, I found you'd written a paltry five pages. That's hardly an heroic output.'

Nick's father looked pained. 'See how tough she is on me.'

Nick was allowed to wriggle out of helping with the dishes that night. He went down to the beach to sit in the moonlight, listening to the waves crash and run with a hiss up the beach to his bare feet.

Heroes always found a way to win through, he thought. He supposed that was a thing you could admire about them. They saw things through to the end and were never deflected from a task.

From the corner of his eye, the boy saw a light travelling up the beach.

He tensed. The light was travelling towards him. It was a battery torchlight, illuminating the face of a man in a tweed cap with clouds of hair at the sides of his head.

It was the doctor.

He was breathing heavily after the tramp along the sand and was as irritable as before. 'Just answer me one question. Have you taken good care of the aeroplane?'

'Yes.'

'We're going in two nights' time. Conditions should be perfect.'

'Conditions where?'

'Near Cape Willoughby lighthouse. You'll need a bit of light. There'll also be a full moon to help.'

'I don't know whether I should go through with it.'

'You can't go back on things now. I've got your money here in an envelope.' He withdrew a yellow envelope from a pocket and opened it to show a wad of crisp, green fifty-dollar bills. He pulled one of the fifties out of the envelope, rustling it temptingly. 'Perhaps you'd like one of these now as a downpayment on your new word processor. You can put it on lay-by and in two days' time you'll have the lot.'

The boy felt his tongue coast around his lips. He wanted the money. He wanted his own word processor. 'No, keep it for now. I want to know something before I agree to do it. What are you going to put on my aeroplane? Drugs?'

'Where am I supposed to stash drugs on a model aeroplane?'

'I don't know.' The boy made a guess. 'In the floats. There's plenty of room in those.'

'If I wanted to fly drugs, I'd use a bigger plane than yours. I'm not putting anything on your plane. You can check it from nose to tail before you fly it. If you can find anything strange on it, I'll give you the two thousand dollars and you can walk away without making the flight.'

'Then why do you insist on using my plane?'

'Because that's the plane you fly best. I told you it's a top secret test of our defences. That's all.'

Kate had taken herself to bed by the time Nick arrived back at the cottage. His father was writing, Beth was making coffee and Popper was fiddling with some fishing gear.

Nick went to his room, opened the curtains and looked at the moon making silvery tracks on the ocean. Somewhere out there were the two islands called The

Pages. He felt The Pages closing around him, squeezing him.

That night he dreamt about it. He was being squeezed by the pages of a book. The pages were heavy as concrete slabs, crushing him beneath their weight. He wished that he was in his grandfather's book instead, the book with gold-edged pages that were as fine and light as insect wings. The keeper was also in his dream, somewhere unseen in the background, watching.

9

The lighthouse

NICK ROSE EARLY, dragging himself out of the bedclothes as if they were the heavy pages of his dream. He looked at a wristwatch. Five-thirty. Good. The word processor was his.

He put on a T-shirt and shorts, took a few things from the bottom of a drawer and went quietly to the word processor in the alcove near the kitchen. He had brought his original disk with him to the island and he loaded the program and fed in the disk. It whirred ruminatively.

He scrolled through some pages that he had written before until he came to the place where he had broken off. Then he opened the notebook that he had been using back on the mainland and began the laborious task of keying in the new material. He did not remember having written so much. When he had completed the transcription, he did not stop there. He continued the story and after that spent time cutting and polishing the work with all the industry of a gem polisher.

Beth came in as the morning sun reached into the

kitchen and lit up his alcove. 'Good morning, Nick. How long have you been working?'

She was wearing a white flowing nightdress. She looked fresh, even in the morning.

'Not long.'

She passed a hand over the top of the monitor. 'Hot. You've been writing for hours.'

Her action struck a spark in Nick. She was checking on him. 'I wanted to finish something,' he said, brusquely. 'I'll probably write all day if I get the chance.'

'No you can't. You're going out with Kate. She was very upset with you for disappearing last night. Where did you go?'

'Down to the beach.'

'In the dark?'

'I wanted to think.'

'Well, you're going on a picnic today,' she announced. 'We arranged it last night. I agreed to pack a picnic basket for you.'

'But I want to write.'

'You're on holiday, Nick. I told you I want you to relax and enjoy yourself.'

Nick flared. If Beth was going to be like this after two weeks of marriage to his father, what would she be like later? It was time to stand up to her. 'You said you weren't going to be my teacher any longer. You're being something worse. You're being a pushy new mother instead.'

That rocked her.

'Nick, I'm sorry. I'm not trying to be pushy. I don't mean to act like the teacher. And I certainly don't want to be a pushy mother. I'm far too new at the job.'

'Then stop blocking me in my writing. Maybe you're afraid I'll compete with your new husband. You're afraid a fifteen-year-old kid will show him up.'

She looked hurt. 'I hope you don't believe that,' she said.

'No, I don't. I'm not good enough to compete, according to you. You think I've got no talent at all. That's why you give me no encouragement and you keep trying to stop me.'

'I think you write very well. You know what else I think. I think you should live life a bit first.'

'That's my decision.'

'Suit yourself, Nick. I never meant to be a stumbling block to you. Is that why you've become resentful about reading books? Because of what I said?'

'I don't want to talk about it any more.' Nick drew back from the subject. He had said enough — more than enough. 'Where am I supposed to be taking Kate on this picnic, anyway?'

'We hadn't quite decided that. We thought we'd give you some choice in the matter.'

'I'd like to go to Cape Willoughby lighthouse.'

'Then the lighthouse it is. There's one more thing: no aeroplanes. Don't look at me like that. It's not my request. It's Kate's. Kate wants some peace and quiet. Now please, Nick, it's too early in the morning for angry words. Let's be friends.'

Beth made breakfast while Nick stored his morning's work on the disk. He switched off, leaving the disk on the computer table so that he could get back to work as soon as the next opportunity arrived.

'Your father has to go to the mainland tomorrow for a meeting,' she told him from the kitchen. 'I'm dropping him at the ferry. He's being collected at the other side.'

The elegantly tapering lighthouse gleamed bone white on the headland against a background of ocean.

'It's whiter than a wedding cake,' Kate said, appreciatively looking up at the windmill-shaped tower.

The wind usually blew strongly here, he guessed. Bushes, distressed by its tug, lay back at an angle as if cowering from it. But there was only a breeze blowing today, fresh and cleansing. Beyond the headland, thousands of miles away, lay the white frozen fortress of Antarctica.

They spread a rug for their picnic on the headland beside a large overhanging bush. 'No noisy aeroplanes,' Kate said. 'Nothing to do but relax.' She lay on the rug, propped on one elbow, breathing in the cool breeze, her eyes shut appreciatively.

She wore a straw hat with a red ribbon around it which looked fine with her red hair. The ribbon fluttered in the breeze.

He was edgy. 'Do you want to go for a walk?' Nick said.

'We've just got here. I want to relax. Can't you relax, Nick?'

'I want to take a look around the lighthouse.'

'Not yet. Sit right here,' she said firmly. 'Explain why you're acting so weirdly. Is it because your father's taken a new wife and you now have a new mum? I hope it isn't because I'm here.'

'No, it isn't you.'

'Then it's your new mum.'

'I don't want to talk about her.'

'Then talk about your real mum.'

'What's to tell? She was with us, then she wasn't. I was young.'

'What do you remember about her?' she said, watching him carefully.

'I only have one lasting picture of her in my mind. And it's not a memory. It's a wedding photo. It used to sit in a frame in my father's study before my father tried to hide it. The photographer had taken a picture of the bride in the church. She had her veil down over her face and it was like looking at her face through clouds. I couldn't quite make out the details. I always thought that the secret of my mother lay behind that veil — that if I could only lift it and look at her I would know her truly. But of course that's impossible, so I guess I'll never know her.'

'That's a lovely thought, Nick. I always knew you were a caring, sensitive boy.'

'Oh no, I'm not. Don't call me that.'

'Don't be embarrassed about having feelings. It's obvious that you miss your mother.'

'Can you miss something you've never had? I don't know. But I know there's a hollow spot inside me. It's sort of dark in there sometimes.'

'Let's not be grim. We're supposed to be on holiday. How about a sandwich?'

They chewed chicken sandwiches that Beth had made for them and washed them down with fresh orange juice.

Later, Nick went for a walk to the lighthouse. He was sorry he had not brought his plane. It would be the ultimate pylon event, flying his plane in a tight circle around the towering white edifice.

He loved pylon racing. He had watched pylon racing contests at aeromodelling championships.

He imagined now that he heard the crackle of a public address sytem and saw pavilions and crowds edging the headland.

He was flying the float plane with five other racers. He banked his Supermarine and went into a turn around the pylon, a twenty-metre-high lighthouse, struggling to hold it steady in the wash of propellers from five other racers that duplicated his manoeuvres inches away from his machine.

Not too high, he told himself, or you'll take the pylon too wide. Not too low or you'll put a wing in. Not that.

The pack broke around it, scattering, and now two of them streaked ahead, his Supermarine and a bright red racer flown by an off duty airforce pilot, Sam Madigan. He was good, very good: a big-shouldered, rugged man with great steady hands that dwarfed the controls on the transmitter hanging on a harness around his leathery neck. Madigan had won the national pylon racing championship three years in a row, until the boy had come along. Over a dozen contests, he had explored the man's every weakness. One thing he had learnt: you did not try to put the pressure on Madigan — he thrived on it. Putting heat and pressure on Madigan was like putting heat and pressure onto a glued joint — it improved the bond and those huge though surprisingly deft fingers became one with the transmitter. Instead, you tried to give him hope and make him relax.

He throttled back the Supermarine in the straight before beginning the next turn, letting the bright red racer flick into the lead. He let Madigan feel the warm breath of success blowing down his neck, waiting for the moment to give his

Supermarine its full, driving strength. Success, especially success earned too easily, would be the undoing of Madigan. As he hoped, Madigan took the next pylon wide.

He snapped the Supermarine into a turn, a fast, pylon-polishing turn around the pylon and now, as he straightened it, he gave it full throttle.

Afterwards when they crowded around him, he shrugged away the praise. 'I got in front of Madigan and kept ahead, that's all.'

The public address system was crackling as happily as bacon and eggs in a frying pan, calling out his name.

It would be a pleasure to fly here in this bright blue sky, Nick thought. But the challenge would be at night. He wondered if he could do it.

That would be the real test of his flying skills. With a full moon and the sweeping beam of the lighthouse, it would be the flight of his dreams. Perhaps he should have a rehearsal.

He noticed that there were a few cottages at the base of the lighthouse and he wondered which one belonged to the lighthouse keeper.

A grey panel van was parked beside the nearest. Was the keeper at home? Nick went to the door and knocked. He thought that he saw a curtain twitch at a window, but nobody came to the door.

A man came around the building from the direction of the lighthouse. Nick recognised the keeper.

'Looking for someone?'

'I was looking for you,' Nick said in surprise. 'Isn't this your house?'

'No, it's one of the guest cottages we rent out to holidaymakers.'

The man joined Nick and smiled his shy, friendly smile. 'I saw you and your friend having a picnic, so I thought I'd come and say hello.' He walked with Nick back to where Kate lay on the blanket. The keeper introduced himself as the keeper; he did not give his name.

'Would you like a chicken sandwich?' Kate said with a welcoming smile, not at all superior.

'No thanks,' he said, 'but I'll sit and chat for a while. Thursday's a quiet day for me. No conducted tours due.' He squatted on the rug and Nick sat nearby.

'Tell us about the lighthouse,' Nick said.

'It's the light at the end of the world,' he said. 'Out there,' he broke to point out to sea, 'lies the white wilderness of Antarctica.'

'But the lighthouse itself?'

'A typical boy's question,' Kate said, making a face.

'It's the oldest in Australia. It has lamps arranged in two banks mounted on a rotating pedestal powered by drive motors and this array turns once every thirty seconds, giving three flashes every thirty seconds.'

'I'm more interested in hearing what it's like being a lightkeeper,' Kate said.

'Generally, it's busy.'

'Busy? All alone in a lighthouse?'

'My life turns with the gymbaled smoothness of the lighthouse lamps. Most lightkeepers are ex-seamen and we run things on nautical lines. I also do weather observations every three hours for the Bureau of Meteorology.'

'Were you ever a seaman?' Nick asked.

'I was once. I had a family, too, but the sea life came between us. My wife left home with our baby boy. I've never seen them since. Maybe that's why I run a lighthouse. Maybe I'm burning a candle for them. . .'

'Or forty thousand candles,' Nick said.

'What a sad and beautiful story. That's two sad stories I've heard today,' Kate said. 'Is that really why you do it?'

'In a way. Maybe my light will guide some other seaman safely back to port so that what happened to me never happens to him. I sometimes wonder if my son also heard the call of the sea and whether, out there in the dark of some night, his eye has fallen on my light without ever knowing it's his father's. We can never be sure of who we're reaching and guiding and that's not just true of lighthouse keepers.'

Nick felt a pang of sympathy for the keeper. He knew what it was to miss the light of a loved one in his life.

'But it's too cheerful a day to think unhappy thoughts.'

'I agree,' Kate said.

'What is it that young people dream about today?' the keeper said. 'What brightens your lives?'

Kate spoke about her love of books. The lean-faced lightkeeper had a power of patience in him and he turned his attention to each of them like a light of steady yet gentle curiosity. 'You like books, too,' he said to Nick, remembering their earlier conversation.

'I like writing.'

'He won't read. He's made a promise to himself never to read again until something happens. . .'

'What happens?'

'That I prove I can write!'

'I remember now. There's somebody who doesn't believe.'

'His English teacher and new mother,' Kate said.

Nick gave her a glare.

'What do you write about?' he asked Nick.

'Heroes and about trying to be like them.'

'I sometimes wonder if real heroes aren't simply the ones who are just themselves through thick and thin.'

'Perhaps, but a life that wasn't spent being here wouldn't be worth reading about.'

'Maybe it wouldn't be worth writing about, either.'

That night, Nick said that he had a headache and wanted to go to bed early. He lay on his bed until he heard the others go to bed, then he got up.

He picked up the Supermarine and slipped the transmitter harness over his head. He made his way stealthily to the front door of the house. The house lay in quietness. They were all in bed. He heard his father give a sneeze in the bedroom. As Nick passed the kitchen, he heard a faint tapping sound coming from the alcove. Typing. Somebody was using the word processor.

He went quietly to check.

Beth sat with her back to him. She wasn't writing. She was reading and correcting text on the screen. Something drew Nick closer. Now he could see. He saw the word 'Flier' printed on the glowing screen.

She was reading *his* work.

Competing feelings squared up inside Nick. At first he felt a flutter of excitement to find her engrossed in his work. She was not idly reading, but scrolling interestedly through the work, bent intently over the glowing screen. Then he felt a feeling of exposure as if she had opened him up to look at his innermost secrets.

He did not know what to do, so he left the house.

He wanted to know the feeling of flying from this place at night. He stood a few hundred metres from the lighthouse. A light breeze tugged at his jacket. It would make flying tricky, but the wind wasn't too strong.

Lightning threw a skeletal hand over a distant part of the sky. He had better make his flight quickly. Using the small light of a pencil torch, he checked his equipment and started up his float plane. Landing would be a bit difficult. He couldn't land it on water at the base of the cliffs, the fall was too steep and, even if he could make it down, the sea was too rough. He would have to land the float plane on the grassy top of the cliff, a bit of a risk, but nothing he hadn't tried before.

Nick made a hand launch into the darkness over the edge of the cliff, fed in some elevator and took it up. The float plane was lit up briefly by the sweeping arc of the lighthouse. A strengthening wind buffeted the Supermarine and he fought with the controls to hold her. The lightning was no longer a hand, but a flickering river of light that ran across the sky towards him. Splashes of rain hit against his leather jacket and against his forehead. He had the feel of it now. He would have to cut this flight short. He put the float plane into a wide turn and brought it back to the cliff's edge. A lash of rain whipped over the clifftop. Nick lowered the aircraft flaps to bring her down, but his eyes were filled with rain, now gaining force.

He knew that he had come in too low even before the float plane, whining back towards him, struck the edge of the cliff. Luckily, it did not fall away, but stuck entangled in a scrubby plant. He made a run to grab it. As his fingers reached it, it slipped and so did he. He lost his footing and tumbled, sliding after it into the sucking black gap below.

10

The rock shelf

HIS FALL WAS BRIEF. He landed heavily on a rock shelf, clutching his float plane by a wingtip. The fall may have been brief, but it was going to be no easy matter climbing back, he discovered. Even in the dark he could see that he was at least ten feet below the rim and up against a wall of rock that was smooth as concrete.

It was hopeless trying to clamber up. He was stuck here until help came. For the night — or longer. The pencil torch had dropped from his pocket. He couldn't even signal for help.

Nick slumped on his shelf of rock, holding his aeroplane. Now the rain came down with a force that nailed him to the rock. He could hear the waves bursting on rocks and churning far below him. If he turned his head to one side he could see the flashes of the lighthouse. Nobody knew he was here. Nobody had any clue of his whereabouts, except one person. A woman who sat at a word processor reading a boy's story.

She was reading it. Would she believe and come looking for him? It was a wild hope. He had written it in the best way he could, as truthfully and with as much feeling as he felt. Perhaps it would reach her and she would feel the truth behind it.

The storm gathered strength. A hand of lightning pointed accusingly at Nick, making him feel even more exposed. Suddenly his life depended on a story. Had he told it well enough?

He clung to a hope as he did to that rock. *Read, Beth, read. Understand, believe,* he willed her.

If she did read it, she did not believe, because she did not come. He felt a laziness creep over him with the cold. An invisible ocean of cold air rolled in above the ocean, washing over him, chilling him right through the leather jacket.

This was how it would end. A boy and a toy aeroplane clinging to a rock and a false hope.

He was no hero. He didn't want to be one. He didn't even know how to pick them. What would he do now? Who would he turn to?

The hero of his life? He pictured the flier's face and saw him grinning at him. It wasn't the flier he had met; it was The Flier he read about in books. The airman rested his hands on Nick's shoulders.

'You can't give up. You've got a job to do.'

'I don't know if I really want to do it.'

His hawkish eyes held a light. 'This is adventure, kid. You may never get another chance like it again. What's the good of having skills if you don't use them? You love adventure and risks, don't you?'

'Yes, but. . .'

'Then have the adventure of your life. Do it!'

'Perhaps not.'

'It's not that simple. You've made an agreement to fly. You can't go and break it.'

'I think I just have.' He shrugged aside the weight of The Flier's hands. They fell limply at The Flier's sides in disappointment.

'Is that the way to treat a friend?'

'I'm not sure you've ever been a friend. You don't care about me; you never did,' he said.

'You expect too much of a hero.'

'You'll never be that to me again.'

'Why, kid? Think of the adventures we've had together and the adventures we can still have in the future.'

With The Flier standing so close, he could smell the smell of a book again.

He was lying on his bed that afternoon at the height of a storm, with rain hammering on their iron roof, and he opened a flying adventure story, going to the heart of the book where the plot was at its thickest. Holding the book to his face, he buried his nose in the converging lines of print. He breathed in the odour of paper and printer's ink, but to him the book did not smell of these things.

He detected a mixture of hot metal, stale flying gear and the pungency of an aviation engine at full throttle.

The adventure of flying.

He remembered flights of imagination he had made in the company of Flite Madison, The Flier, a renegade pilot who flew the world in a float plane, putting down where he chose on the Amazon, the Zambesi, the Nile, Mississippi, Murray River or in some Pacific island cove.

'Stay with me,' The Flier said.

'Sorry, Flier. I think I've had enough of you.'

'We must stick together,' he said. 'We'll fly to new adventures, anywhere you like. Where shall we go? We can fly to Africa, to the Zambesi. Or to the Nile. You liked it there. Look into my eyes,' he said. 'I'll show you the views of the world and adventures only I can take you to.'

They were on the Amazon. Their cockpit was filled with Spanish treasure and headhunters were paddling after them in war canoes, firing darts from their blowguns. They were going downwind, impossible for take-off.

The Flier threw their float plane into a violent turn then raced back between the canoes. The headhunters let fly.

Darts sprouted from their fuselage like spines on an echidna's back. . .

'Stop,' he said to The Flier. 'That's enough. It won't work this time.' He broke the hold of his hawkish eyes.

Popper had told him about a different hero. He remembered him now.

'An agent who works from within,' Popper said. 'He went by a codename, Light of the World, and he lived by his wits, surrounded by enemies. In the end he sacrificed himself for others. He's the only hero who promised never to leave us. He'll be with us until the end of time and you can always call on him. I've got his book. You should read it some time.'

He remembered the book. He had looked at it once. Popper kept it by his bedside. It was a battered black book with tissue-thin, gold-edged pages that were fine as insects' wings and almost transparent. The thought calmed him.

Nick was exposed to more than the wind, the rain, the dark and the lightning. He was exposed to the knowledge of his own stupidity. He had made a bad mistake in coming here tonight, but he had probably been saved from making an even greater mistake.

Was it worth making a bad choice simply because it offered experience?

A light came to him and shone above him in the storm.

'Help!' Nick called.

The light came nearer. It wasn't Beth. It was a young, sinewy man in a yellow raincoat with a lantern. In the light, Nick saw a face with hair like windblown straw. It was the lightkeeper. He saw a narrowing of surprise in the downturned eyes.

'It's the boy who flies.'

'And crashes,' Nick said ruefully.

'I'll be back with a rope, son.'

He left the light on the clifftop to comfort Nick and came back with a coil of rope. How had he known to come here?

The keeper made a loop in the rope and lowered it to Nick. Nick climbed into it, hooking it under his arms. Still holding his aeroplane, he allowed himself to be heaved to the top.

'You're all right now,' the keeper said, patting Nick's shoulder.

'How did you know that I was in trouble?'

'I saw some small flashes of light earlier. Almost forgot about it, but something kept worrying me about it. Eventually I decided to take a look.'

The light from his pencil torch. The lightkeeper had seen it, small as it was. 'Thanks for looking out,' Nick said. 'And thanks for coming. I didn't think anyone had seen me.'

'There's not much that I miss from up there,' the keeper said, and he cast a glance at the lighthouse. 'Come to the cottage and we'll get you warmed up.'

He took Nick to one of the cottages, the furthest away from the lightouse.

The cottage was warmed by a fire. He covered Nick in a blanket, made some hot chocolate in a big yellow mug and sat beside him. 'Now tell me what you're up to, son.'

But he wasn't ready to tell yet. 'I was just practising some night flying,' he said.

They were all peacefully asleep when the keeper drove Nick home. He slipped undetected into his bedroom and slept.

In spite of his ordeal, he awoke early. He went to the word processor. He wanted to complete the story. There was a final part to add. He loaded the program and his disk and scrolled through to the bottom.

He received a mild, but not totally unpleasant shock. Beth had written a message at the bottom of his story:

I do take an interest. I discovered your story while I was checking your father's disks. I won't pretend I haven't read it; I have, and I'm finding it very exciting. I can't wait to see what the boy does next. Hope you're not angry. Just think of me as your editor. Beth.

It almost made up for the night before and for a lot of other things, yet she had not believed.

The boy sat down to write about the things he knew best of all — his feelings. He wrote about what he had lived through, especially about the time on the rocks.

of all — with his emotions. He broke out of story and spoke as one person to another:

To my reader:
I am sorry if I have not made you believe. I have tried to fill the pages with events, hoping to sweep you along in a high wind of adventure. But the harder I blow, the more you cling to your doubts. Perhaps the lesson to learn is like the one told in the nursery school fable about the sun and the wind.

One day the sun and the wind saw a man in a coat walking across a plain. The sun and the wind, who were rivals, engaged in a bet about their powers to affect the man. 'I'll bet I can make the man take off his coat quicker than you can,' the wind boasted. (Perhaps the coat was a leather flying jacket with zips and pockets in all the right places.) The wind tried first. The sun went behind clouds and the wind sprang up to test his power. He blew and blew so hard that he almost rolled the man back like a leaf. Instead of taking off his jacket, though, the man ran the zip of his jacket higher under his chin and leaned into the wind to walk against its pressing force. The wind rose to a shriek. The man just huddled deeper into his jacket. The wind was powerless.

Then it was the sun's turn. The sun came out from behind the clouds and smiled warmly on the walking man. The man brightened. He started to whistle. Soon he was unzipping his jacket. The sun rose higher into the sky, shining directly on the man. The man slowed, then stopped and peeled off his jacket. It was too good a day to go covered. He walked on happily in the sunshine.

Is my situation like the wind and the sun? If blowing doesn't work, perhaps the warmth of feelings can peel off the layers of disbelief.

This is what I felt as I lay on the rocks.

When he had written this, he wrote an ending, because a real author, even if that author was only a boy, should never leave a story without an ending.

11

Solarskin

NOW THAT HE HAD DECIDED not to go through with it, he knew that he must return the valuable float plane to the authorities on the mainland. It wouldn't be easy. The doctor and his people were bound to be watching and would never let him leave the island with it.

The boy's father was going over on the ferry that day and that, he decided, was his only way out, but he couldn't simply walk onto the ferry. He couldn't hide the aircraft under his arm. It had a wingspan of just under two metres and it weighed over four kilos. They would see it and try to stop him. He would have to think of another plan.

It left very few options. If he couldn't carry it over on the crossing and if the Backstairs Passage was too far to fly across, then there was only one, daring solution.

He would need the help of the girl.

They were watching at the wharf although he did not see them at first. The boy and his father said goodbye to the woman who drove them to the jetty. He and his father walked up the gangplank to board the catamaran ferry. The boy carried a small satchel over one shoulder. That must have reassured them.

The crew of the catamaran ferry cast off and, with a rumble of its twin engines, it pulled off from the jetty. His father waved to the woman.

The boy went to the open deck at the stern. He swung the satchel off his shoulder, opened it and dug inside to remove his radio transmitter. He pulled out the two-metre-long whip aerial and gave the girl hidden on the shore a wave.

He hoped it would work. He had shown the girl what to do and how to launch the aircraft by hand, smoothly in a glide that was level with the ground.

There it came, a soft grinding sound like a mosquito. The tiny blue-and-white float plane left the cover of the trees and came out over the water. The boy fed in some elevator and took it up.

He was not prepared for how quickly they reacted. The woman on the jetty was still walking to her car when the doctor ran along the wharf and jumped into a speedboat moored near the end. He was probably in radio contact with others on the island.

The boy watched the low, white jetboat race out after them, dodging to avoid the wake of the ferry. He wondered what the doctor hoped to achieve. He could hardly stop the ferry, nor could he board her. The doctor did not try. He seemed content to hang back, waiting. He cruised alongside at half speed, staring at the boy.

They were twenty minutes out of Penneshaw and would reach their destination, Cape Jervis, in another forty minutes. Then the doctor's plan became clear. A small red biplane grew on the horizon.

It confirmed what the boy had dreaded, but had known all along. The flier was in cahoots with the doctor. He had tried to influence the boy, to encourage him to go through with an illegal flight.

Other passengers gathered around the boy to watch as the biplane drew closer. It flew over the ferry once and tilted inquisitively to take a look at the boy. He recognised the flier sitting alone in the rear cockpit. He gave the boy a wave. Then he came back towards the boy's float plane and went into a dive to engage.

The boy had sometimes dreamed of flying against him and he wasn't going to run just yet. He fed in some elevator and sent his float plane up. The red biplane swooped across his vision, throwing a shadow on the deck of the ferry before it went up into the sun. Passengers on the stern deck gasped. The boy banked to follow. A biplane is pretty manoeuvrable, but against a model it was like an eagle trying to catch a darting blowfly. The boy came out of the sun and flew all over him, although he was careful to avoid the wash from the biplane's propeller and the blade itself that could chop his Supermarine into a puff of sawdust. The flier tried to swat him with a roll of his wingtips, but the boy banked out of his way, did an Inside Loop and came up underneath him.

An elderly man standing beside the boy applauded. The boy wondered where his father had got to. Typical parents; they never paid any attention when you were doing something brilliant. His father was probably having a cup of coffee and reading a paper in the canteen while his son engaged in a thrilling aerial combat.

The boy was feeling pretty pleased with himself, but he had underestimated the flier. Once he saw what he was up against, it was his turn to show off. He could fly. He threw the red biplane around in a way that he had no right to do and in a way that showed little respect for the old barnstormer. The boy gulped and climbed downstairs to skim along the wavetops. The speedboat changed course and made a run to head him off. That wasn't going to help the boy.

They could get him in the air and they could get him in the water. What could he do? He saw a military Hercules aircraft lumbering across the sky. Pity its rear cargo doors weren't open, he thought; he could pop in and land there snugly.

He kept looking. Out on the horizon, closer than the first time he had seen it, stood the grey, steel mountain of the Nimitz aircraft carrier. Did he dare make a landing on the decks of a nuclear powered aircraft carrier? He fed in more throttle and headed towards it.

The red biplane guessed his intentions and tried to blow him into the water with the wash of her propellers. The boy waited until the giant sawmill was almost on his tail before hauling back on the stick and going into a huge Inside Loop that put him on the biplane's tail. It wasn't all that smart a move, he discovered, even though it was neatly executed. The wash from the biplane's props hit him like a wall and he struggled to keep the float plane under control.

Aboard the aircraft carrier, radar eyes on a detached lattice radar mast swept the area. He wondered if some naval radar operator sitting in the phosphorescent glow of a screen could see his float plane as a chip of blinking light. It would certainly see the biplane chasing him.

The boy could sense the giant tensing. He could imagine the hum and whine of machinery as deck-edge lifts raised gleaming fighters into the sunlight. He saw a figure running on the flight deck.

The biplane guessed what he was planning. He heard a change in the pitch of its engine as it slowed. You didn't just cold-call on a Nimitz class aircraft carrier. It was armed with twenty-four Mk 29 Sea Sparrow missiles, two fighter and three attack squadrons, not to mention around thirty other types of aircraft. But the kid kept going.

Would a Sea Sparrow missile fizz up from the deck and stream towards his plane at any second? The biplane altered course and went into a circle to watch him. Men on the deck of the aircraft carrier were pointing up at the approaching float plane. The boy climbed a little before bringing it into a landing attitude. It was like a fly coming down to land on a floating table mountain. The flight deck of a Nimitz class aircraft carrier offered plenty of room for landing. It was so long that you could hold the Olympic 100 metre track event on the deck, starting with the first heat and second heats and then the final race, end to end, and there'd still be room at the finish for a cheering crowd.

A man on the flight deck ran out in the path of the float plane. He wore a luminous yellow jacket and was swinging two objects like table tennis racquets. The float plane was almost on top of him when he took a swat at it, missing widely. Ha, the boy jeered; you need a better backhand than that to hit me!

He brought the float plane down on the deck on its floats. Landing on an armoured deck without wheels did not make for a soft landing, but it wasn't nearly so bad as flying into a cliff face — and at least the plane was home, safely in the hands of the Western alliance.

But would that be the right ending, he wondered.

The boy was walking on the beach when the doctor came for him in a grey panel van. He stopped on the road a small distance from the cottage. The doctor climbed out of the driver's seat and waved to him.

The boy had toyed with the idea of running away. Now it was too late. But he couldn't let them have the plane. He decided to play along with them.

He waved back.

'Get the plane and your things,' the doctor called. 'We're going tonight.'

'Wait here,' the boy said.

He went into the house. Beth and Kate were baking in the kitchen. He had hoped that they would be out. It made things difficult. He decided that he would have to draw the doctor safely away from them.

'Are you staying home now?' Beth said.

'No, I'm about to fly.'

'First try one of our doughnuts,' Kate said.

'Sorry, not now.'

'Why's he in such a hurry to go flying?' Kate said.

He collected his plane, his transmitter and his flying jacket and left through Popper's back door. He would go to the lighthouse keeper for help. It was his only hope. Perhaps the keeper had a radio and could call for help. Getting there through bush on foot was going to be difficult carrying an aeroplane. In the backyard of the cottage, he swung the transmitter harness over his neck and started the float plane. He would run with it flying above him, drawing the doctor away from Beth and Kate, and then try to lose the doctor before making his way to the lighthouse keeper's cottage.

He vaulted a low fence that surrounded the cottage and ran into the scrub, staying in contact with the plane above him, putting it into wide circles. The doctor saw and heard the plane. The boy heard the panel van's engine kick into life. The car followed on and took a dirt road that ran to the edge of the scrub.

The boy ran, bushes and trees sliding past in a blur, his fingers manipulating the control levers. The float plane seemed to be enjoying the chase up there, he thought. He wished he had the same view it did. Where was the doctor?

Was he gaining on him? The aircraft stayed firmly in his control as if he were running with a kite on a string.

He kept going until he reached a clearing where he brought the float plane softly down on some thick grass, killing the engine. He listened for the running footsteps of the doctor. The silence swarmed in his ears after the whine of the engine. He heard nothing. For safety, he decided to wait there a little longer before running on.

He knocked on the door to the lighthouse keeper's cottage. Something was wrong. He sensed it.

'Don't stand there. Go right in,' the flier said behind him. 'We've been waiting for you.'

'How did you get here?' the boy said, twisting. The flier, dressed just as he remembered him in leather flying gear, smiled.

'I fly, remember.'

The door to the keeper's cottage opened. The doctor stood there. The flier gave the boy a soft shove from behind, propelling him inside. The doctor took the float plane from Nick as he passed.

They had the keeper tied to a kitchen chair.

Nick took off the transmitter harness. He also took off his leather jacket and held it out to the flier.

'Here's your jacket back.'

'No, you keep it. It wouldn't fit me anyway.'

Nick let it fall to the floor. 'You were mixed up in this plan of the doctor's all along. You were the pilot who was supposed to fly my plane out, but you couldn't fly because of your injured hand. Am I right?'

'Something like that, but don't bother your head with that stuff now. You've got to prepare yourself for a bit of flying tonight.'

'Let the keeper go,' the boy said, 'or I won't fly anything.'

'You'll fly,' the doctor said, 'or your friend will. Over the cliff,' he said unpleasantly.

There was no warmth in the keeper's house this time. There was no fire burning in the fireplace as there had been when the keeper had brought him here after the storm and given him a bright yellow mug of hot chocolate.

The doctor and the flier had rented one of the lighthouse cottages and had been staying here all along. He remembered seeing a grey panel van parked outside one of the cottages and seeing a curtain twitch when he had knocked at the door.

'Sit down,' the doctor told the boy, putting the float plane on a table. The boy chose a chair near the keeper.

'Why is he gagged? Does he have to be? I want to speak to him.'

The doctor shrugged. It made no difference now. They had the boy and the float plane. The flier arranged himself lazily on a couch, resting one boot carelessly on the green fabric. He tried to look relaxed, but he avoided the boy's condemning glare.

The doctor removed the cloth that gagged the keeper's mouth.

'I'm sorry I've brought this on you through my stupidity,' the boy said to the keeper. 'These people want me to fly something out to sea in my aeroplane.'

He looked at the flier and then at the lighthouse keeper. There were dark shadows like caves in the flier's face. The lightkeeper sat near a window that lit his lean, sinewy form and calm face. There was no fear in the keeper's face. He looked concerned for the boy. The boy wondered how he could be that way at a time like this. Looking out for others. It was his job. The keeper watched the boy like a man observing faroff lights for signs of distress.

Who was the real hero, this quietly dedicated man, or the reckless flier who lounged on the couch like a fighter pilot resting between dangerous exploits?

'You can tell me about the aeroplane,' the boy said to the doctor. 'It doesn't matter now. What's on it?'

'Don't tell him,' the flier put in.

The boy felt his anger burn. 'Haven't you kept enough from me already? Must you go on fooling me to the end?'

'I don't think he's trying to fool you,' the doctor said in an irritable voice. 'I think he's trying to protect you. I'm afraid our flying friend has developed a soft spot for his young protege. I don't think he's ever had anyone look up to him before. You want to know? Then I'll tell you.'

'Don't,' the flier said. 'Once they know. . .'

'So you are growing sentimental,' he said to the flier. 'Try thinking of the money we've already paid you and what's still to come — money for work you can't do properly yourself because you were careless and cut your hand.'

The flier looked away.

'What's on my plane?' the boy said.

'Dope.'

'Drugs? Where?'

'Dope, dope. The aeroplane is coated with a revolutionary dope, a substance called Solarskin. Solarskin is as light as plastic, but has a tensile strength five times greater than steel. So you see, it is a rather special plane you have there.'

It answered a lot of the boy's questions, especially about how his aeroplane had survived an argument with a cliff face and come through without a dent. 'Are you really a doctor?'

'Yes, I am a doctor. I am a scientist engaged in polymer research.'

'Plastics.'

'Reinforced plastics. Do you know anything about reinforced plastics?'

'Only that in some cases plastics are used where metal was once used.'

'We shall explore the universe in plastic rockets, take my word for it. The future is plastic. We shall live in plastic houses, fly in plastic aeroplanes, sail in plastic ships, but very different plastics from the ones you know. Around the globe, scientists like me are engaged in designing new thread-like molecules which will give us the plastic of tomorrow. Solarskin is such a plastic.'

'You designed Solarskin?'

'No, a colleague beat me to it, but I was part of the team and managed to steal a small sample,' he said.

'And Des from the Hobby Hangar put it on my aircraft?'

'Exactly. He changed sides.'

'What will they do with it?'

'Analyse it. Recreate the substance. The next time you hear about Solarskin it will be on the skin of an enemy aircraft flying into your country. Or on a submarine which will cruise into a sensitive port. Solarskin has staggering properties. Its high stress applications are endless. A few outer coatings of Solarskin form an exoskeleton of enormous strength. Yet it is lighter than metal. That means it would actually increase an aircraft's payload while increasing its structural strength.'

Was the boy's float plane, covered with Solarskin, now stronger than steel? It explained the tough, shiny new finish of the surface. The doctor went on: 'Being a plastic it has a higher resistance to corrosion than a metal. But it has an even more compelling advantage. Your little aeroplane is invisible.'

'But I can see it.'

'Invisible to radar. We knew before we began that glass reinforced plastics were less reflective to radar beams than metal. Solarskin, however, is all but transparent to radar frequencies.'

'Who are we giving it to?'

'There are some secrets I must keep.'

'Happy now?' the flier said.

The boy locked glances with him.

'I believed in you,' he said.

'Sorry, kid.'

'You're not a hero; you're just a model aeroplane flier.'

'Among other things. I fly radio-controlled aeroplanes for relaxation. I told you I can fly anything. Big planes, little planes, jet planes, paper planes. You name it, I fly it.'

12

The decision

THEY STOOD ON THE CLIFFTOP in the dark, the doctor beside him and the flier somewhere further back in the darkness, keeping watch.

The breeze had calmed and a full moon threw a trail of splintered light on a gently swelling sea.

'You'd better get ready,' the doctor said. 'And you'd better be thorough. No mistakes. Check everything. Put these reflector strips on the wings.' He handed the boy some strips of adhesive red paper.

He held a torchlight while the boy stuck the strips to the wings. The boy went through preliminary checks, checking the transmitter and the control surfaces. This was the serious side of the sport, the tinkering with the complex that held an appeal for a certain kind of boy. One oversight — a disconnected plug or push rod — would be the end.

'All fine,' the boy said. 'When do we go?'

'We're waiting for a signal.' He switched off the torch, plunging them into semidarkness. From where they stood he could hear the surf and even glimpse the waves marching in against the jagged rocks at the foot of the cliff. The glaring yellow sweep of Cape Willoughby light probed the sky intermittently. *The boy peered into the night, hunting for lights. Somewhere out there in the moonlit sea lay the sleek, deadly form of a submarine. A submarine sent by which foreign power? And he was going to make contact with it. The boy felt a crawling sense of revulsion as if he were about to brush against something loathsome like a spider's web.*

The boy ran his fingers over the smooth surface of the float plane, testing its strength. He tried to bend the tailplane and, although he felt his fingers whiten with the pressure, it resisted his efforts. Next he tried to scratch the fuselage with a fingernail. It was as hard as glass.

A coating of Solarskin had done this to his aeroplane. Dope. He had been one all right. He should have guessed. It would be worth a great deal to any country. And tonight it would fly out of the boy's life. What possibilities for his country would fly out with it?

'There they are.'

The boy followed the doctor's line of vision and felt excitement bunch up in him like a fist. There it was, a white flashing light, a few kilometres offshore.

'Go,' the doctor said to the boy. 'Land as near as you can.'

The doctor sent a flash out to the submarine. The light from his torch found an answering glow in the reflector strips on the float plane's wings.

'You'll have to help me,' the boy said. It would be a hand launch. He held the plane out to the doctor. 'Hold it tight until I give you the signal to launch, then push it into the air, not too fast and in a smooth level action.'

He started the engine. It quivered in the doctor's hands, eager to be airborne. He advanced the throttle.

He saw the flash of the lighthouse and a picture of the keeper came into his mind. There's a difference between having skills and choosing good causes, the keeper had said.

'Now.'

The doctor released the float plane in a fluid launch. The boy gave it more throttle, bringing the little engine angrily to life. It sailed over the cliff and out above the sheer drop.

Then a finger prodded his brain. Diving to one side, he slammed it into a zoom and then hauled back smartly on a control lever.

Then he ran.

The doctor gave a shout and loosed a shot. A black wind slammed past the boy's face. In a vicious loop, the float plane came whining back upon them, aimed at the figure of the doctor. The man dropped moments before it swept overhead. The boy had to keep in contact with the plane or he might still lose it.

The lighthouse.

If he could keep it in a circle around the lighthouse, it would be lit by the flashing beam.

The doctor sprang to his feet to give chase. He must have dropped his gun when he fell. He wasn't shooting. He was looking for it.

The boy ran back between the bushes. They leaned over at a crazy angle like an abstract painting in the moonlight. Where was the flier? He headed the Supermarine in the direction of the lighthouse. He put the plane in a wide circle around the structure.

He ducked down, crouching behind a large bush. With fingertips on the controls, he felt for the aircraft. Where was it? It should be in a circle passing in front of the lighthouse at any second. Perhaps it was too low. The boy had estimated that the focal plane of the lighthouse was some eighty metres above sea level. He flew blindly in another circle, increasing height.

There it was. The flash of Cape Willoughby lighthouse hit its gleaming fuselage, like searchlights hitting a bomber. He half expected to see a trail of tracer bullets streak up to attack it.

A bullet came instead, shot wildly into the darkness near him, and a torchlight began to circle him. The doctor was driving him towards the edge of the headland. There was no way to get past him. Another shot convinced the boy of the hopelessness of trying to break through. He left the cover of the bushes and drew back to the cliff's edge. He was nearing the edge of the headland now, closer to the sea. He was still in contact with the circling float plane.

The doctor was closing the gap between them. The boy reached the edge of the headland and clambered down rocks. He couldn't go any further, he thought, looking down at the foam-laced rocks at the foot of the cliff.

He took cover behind some rocks and prepared to make his stand. He took the plane out of its holding pattern around the lighthouse and brought her in. He could see the doctor coming towards him, gun in hand. The boy banked the float plane, then dropped its nose in a shallow, fast dive that took it sawmilling down to the advancing man.

The doctor saw the danger and dived to the ground, loosing off a shot at the plane. Nick took evasive action. The model flicked past the doctor's head. He hauled back on the stick, looping it back for another strike.

Then a cloud passed over the face of the moon.

Now he was flying blind, except for the regular sweeping flashes of the Cape Willoughby light.

He put the model through a tight turn, grateful for the hairline accuracy of its controls. Not too low, don't put a wing in. That would be disaster. How high was it above the ground? Was that the shadowy figure of the doctor raising himself? The boy looked pleadingly up at the moon veiled by cloud. Stay there, hide me. Where was the aeroplane exactly? Another few moments and the veil would move aside. Seconds. It was then that the obvious occurred to him. If he could not see the plane, neither could the doctor. They could only hear it.

The boy put the float plane in a steep climb. It whined up above the headland. How near was the doctor now? How much time would he have? He flattened himself behind the rock. The beam of the lighthouse swept overhead. It was followed by a smaller beam from a handtorch. The doctor had seen his hiding place and was playing the light over the pile of rocks.

Miraculously, the doctor went past the boy towards the edge. Did he think the boy was further down or that he had fallen over? The veil of cloud was almost drawn from the moon.

The boy cut back the power, quietening the screaming engine.

He heard it splutter as its powerplant almost died. He fed in a little more juice to keep it alive. He could still hear the plane, but it sounded far away now. The sounds of the night closed in, the sea dashing rocks at the base of the headland. He heard the doctor swear.

The float plane dropped in a tail slide. Recovering an aircraft from a tail slide was one of the hardest exercises in flying and not one of the boy's favourites, even in daylight. In near darkness it was getting close to the impossible. He let the aircraft drop, trying to guess its height. How far was it from the headland? Had he waited too long already? Maybe he should pull out of it before he ploughed into the ground.

It came at once. The moon emerged from the cloud. The sweeping light of the lighthouse hit them. The boy sent out a pulse that turned up the model's power and he fought with all of her controls in an effort to right her. The Cape Willoughby light moved on. Darkness again. The doctor probed the sky with the torch in an effort to see the plane, but the thin beam of light stared weakly into the night. Too late he glimpsed the plane in the next sweep of light from the lighthouse. Like a bird of ill omen, the tiny aircraft swooped. The boy gave it full throttle. It screamed out of the sky. The float plane hit the man with a smothered, stinging sound like a giant hornet sinking its sting into flesh. He fell back, firing another shot.

The aircraft went into a somersault over the edge of the cliff. The boy struggled to regain control. Had the blow damaged its receivers? It went twisting out to sea.

Stunned, blinded it seemed and now firing at random, the doctor stepped off the headland. As he dropped, he made one last grab for the edge. Then he went soundlessly into the waves below.

The model was still airborne in a flat yawing spin, wildly out of control. The boy tried to straighten it out. He added a mental signal to the one that went out from his transmitter. Come on, float plane, answer me.

There. A faint change in the note of its engine signalled a response.

That was when the flier got to the boy. 'Fly it back here, kid.'

'I won't.'

'Then let me have it. Give me control,' he said. He held out his hand, a hand that was leathery and big as a baseball glove. The boy took a step back. 'Give me control,' the flier said again.

It was time to give up. He had tried his best. What else could he be expected to do? Much too much had happened. It would be so easy to do what this man said, to hand over control. The light from Cape Willoughby sent its pulsing flash out into the night and the boy saw the flashing light as a sign.

He slipped the radio transmitter harness off his head. Then he twisted and spun with it like a discus thrower and hurled the transmitter and harness off the cliff and into the breakers below. Without control, how far would the plane go? Twenty, thirty kilometres? Would it ever be found again?

A car arrived, its headlights spilling light over the cliff.

'You win,' the flier said, his shoulders slumping. 'You're quite a flier. And quite a kid.' Then he simply walked away into the night.

Beth came to him as he was busy writing on the computer.

'Well, did you go through with the flight or didn't you?' There was a note of anxiety in her voice.

'Did *I*?' he said.

'I mean "the boy",' she said. 'Sorry, you almost had me going there.'

'Did I?' he said, his tone changing to delight. 'Well, I suppose that's something.'

'You can be pretty convincing, Nick.'

That was all Nick wanted to hear. He smiled.

'Let's go and read a book on the beach,' Nick said after breakfast.

Kate almost dropped the plate she was ferrying to the kitchen. 'You're actually going to read?'

'Why not?'

'But I thought you were going to dedicate yourself to writing?'

'I can write. I proved it. And if I can write, then I can read.'

'But you didn't bring any books with you. Do you want to read one of mine?'

'No thanks. Not Judy Blume again.'

He knocked on Popper's door. Popper was gathering his fishing gear to go fishing.

'Come in, Nick.'

'I wanted to borrow a book, Popper.'

'Any particular book?'

'You know the one.'

He pointed to the battered black volume that sat on Popper's bedside drawer, the one with gold edges and pages as fine as insect wings. Popper gave it to him with a surprised smile on his face.

Nick opened the book at its heart and lifted it to his nose. It smelt of adventures, too, but of a different kind; also of truth and of wisdom.

'I don't say this is the only book I'll read from now on, but I have an idea it will change every book I ever read in the future.'

'Count on it,' Popper said.

He went with Kate to the beach.

'I always knew you were a sensible boy,' she said.

Beth intercepted Nick later that day as he walked along the shore.

'I'm sorry I doubted you, Nick. I was wrong about you. I think you are a born writer after all. You shouldn't ever stop.' She walked beside him, stepping in the waves that ran up the white sand.

'I'm also a born reader. And I won't ever stop reading either, I promise you. And you were right about another thing. I shouldn't give up living for writing.'

'Good,' she said. 'Keep a part of yourself free to enjoy creation. To gather the beautiful living flowers. To appreciate this sea that we can feel washing around our ankles. This cool sand that we can feel between our toes. This sky above us both. This whole island and this whole world. And the people you care about. Like lovely, cool-eyed Kate.'

'And you,' Nick said, a little shyly.

'Thankyou, Nick,' Beth said, genuinely pleased. 'I like you, too, even more as I come to understand you. I think you and I will be friends.'

'I think there's a good chance,' he said.

'I can't replace your mother. I won't even try. I'll always be me, but I'll try to be a friend.'

'I'm not worried about replacing my mother,' he said. 'It's my English teacher I'm worried about. Who is going to replace you? What will I do when you go? The headmaster Mr Parry is not my idea of a fair swap.'

'You'll do fine,' she said. 'There's one thing I must ask you. It's about your story. How much of what you wrote was true? You didn't actually fly a vintage plane on your own, did you? And I know you didn't land your model float plane on the deck of a Nimitz class aircraft carrier. And did somebody really try to skyjack your plane from a cabin cruiser?'

'That's for a writer to know and a reader to guess,' Nick said with a secret smile.

Kate waved to them. He waved back. His father came down to the beach to join them, wearing his swimming costume.

'Enough writing for me,' he said. 'I've finished for now. It's time to start living.'

He was right, especially when the island air smelled of the spice of sea, sunshine and exotic growing things, of real-life adventures waiting to be lived.